GRAVENFROST

Peter Hammarberg

This is a work of fiction. Names, characters, places, and
incidents are products of the author's imagination are
used fictitiously and are not to be construed as real. Any
resemblance to actual events, locales, organizations, or
persons, living or dead, is entirely coincidental.

ISBN: 978-0-9908397-2-9

Cover art by: Glenn Barr
www.glbarr.com

Art directed by: Robert Paul Nixon
www.robertpaulnixon.com

The house it shakes and creaks with fear
The fear this time, we've really had it
But hey, I don't care
If death is hanging in the air
'Cause I knew I had it coming
When they handed out good luck
I wasn't there.

-Dom Kreep, "SuperNova"

SPECIAL THANKS

To my wife, Christina, for being the brains and the brawn of our outfit. I couldn't do it without you, and quite frankly wouldn't want to. Robert Nixon, who wholeheartedly supported my creeping descent into madness, and for his expertise in all things horror. Your art and friendship have been an amazing inspiration. Glenn Barr, for bringing Doyle to life with art so amazing that if people judge this book by its cover, we're golden! Shelley Mascia of *Shelley's Editing Services*, for her early-draft technical edits. Shannon Cox, Angel Larcom, and Sean Schmidenberg, for being my test subjects—your input and support have been invaluable.

And if you're reading this?

Thank you most of all.

For the haunted.

1
CHILDREN OF THE GRAVE

OFFICIAL FBI TRANSCRIPT
CASE: "DEVIL'S DOMICILE" MULTIPLE
HOMICIDE
DEBRIEFING: AGENT ROBERT DOYLE
CONDUCTOR: AGENT REBECCA REMENDER
SEPTEMBER 24, 2013
1500 HOURS

[RECORDING BEGINS]

ARR: FEDERAL AGENT REBECCA REMENDER.
POST-OP INTERVIEW OF SPECIAL AGENT
ROBERT DOYLE.
ARD: BOBBY.
ARR: COME AGAIN?
ARD: YOU CAN CALL ME BOBBY, OR DOYLE.
NO NEED FOR THE SPECIAL AGENT
BULLSHIT. THIS IS A FRIENDLY
INTERROGATION, RIGHT, BECKY?
ARR: DEBRIEFING, AGENT DOYLE. AND
NOBODY CALLS ME BECKY.
ARD: OKAY. SORRY. IM STILL GONNA ASK
YOU OUT FOR DRINKS AFTER THIS.
ARR: WHAT ARE YOU DOING?
ARD: ASKING YOU OUT?

ARR: NO. WHY ARE YOU TAKING CIGARETTES OUT?
ARD: A FIX. IF I'M GOING TO BE TELLING YOU THIS TALE OF HORROR AND PERIL, DADDY'S GONNA NEED TO BURN ONE. OR TEN.
ARR: THIS IS A NON-SMOKING FACILITY AGENT DOYLE.
ARD: BOBBY.
ARR: I UNDERSTAND AND APRECIATE THE ORDEAL YOU'VE JUST GONE THROUGH, BUT PLEASE, ALL I ASK IS THAT WE GET THIS STARTED. THE SOONER WE DO, THE SOONER WE'RE OUT OF HERE.
ARD: GETTING DRINKS.
ARR: WE ARE NOT GETTING--
ARD: --GRAVENFROST, MAINE. THAT'S THE LITTLE NUGGET OF HEAVEN THE AGENCY SENT ME TO.

Located a mile-and-a-half off the coast of Machiasport, Maine—it's a place steeped in historical folklore and local bullshittery. Gravenfrost is said to be one of the most haunted places in the world. Why, you ask? Good question. Legend (Wikipedia) has it, that the forty-nine-and-change square miles of earth was puked out of the Atlantic like a Jäger-soaked frosted bear claw. In 1633, the English discovered that the Passamaquoddy natives had used it to bury their disgraced dead. Think about that for a second. You were such a horrible person, your own tribe would canoe your dead ass over a mile away to plant you in the ground so the corruption wouldn't poison the rest of the land. The English didn't grasp that concept. They said, *Hey, that's a cool idea. Who wants to bury the dead right next door? We should, I dunno, bury our homies there too. For, like, sanitary reasons.* The Passamaquoddy didn't have a name for the place. They didn't want to give it an identity, because that would give it power. But the Brits? Those guys love giving places names. Newcastle Upon Tyne, Huyton-

2

With-Roby. Silly geese, the lot of them. They found that the ground was far too hard to bury folks in the winter months, so instead, they would just leave the bodies right there and get to them come spring. Even as early as October, they would see frost forming on the gravestones. I imagine they'd say, *By jove, I do believe I see graven frost across the bay.* Then the other guy chuffs and says, *Quite right, quite right.* Then they have tea. The name stuck. When spring came, they'd bury whatever was left. This practice, of course, started a whole slew of stories of people watching the dead shamble around.

The island played a huge part in the Salem Witch Trials, and the Malleus Maleficarum frenzy sweeping the Top 40 charts at the time. Those who could, fled to Gravenfrost to hide from the bible-humping cock waffles, knowing full well that nobody would be nuts enough to follow—and it was big enough a place to hide even if they did. Then the French came around and everyone was stabbing everyone else. Blah, blah, blah—history stuff. More bodies were piled up and planted.

Cue the Revolutionary War.

The Machias, Machiasport, and Gravenfrost area was where the first naval battle took place, so woo-hoo. When the American militia used the far side of the island to build a fort, they discovered an abandoned series of small huts and shacks and an IHOP. It was a ghost town. Where did everybody go? Can I keep this bitchin' boombox? Nobody knew the answers to those important questions. They built a half-assed battery called Fort Beacon and blah, blah, blah, we all know how the Revolution turned out by the lack of the letter "u" in color.

3

I need a smoke.

ARR: I'M SORRY, AN IHOP?
ARD: YOU KNOW HOW MUCH YE OLDE
AMERICANS LOVED THEIR CHOCOLATE CHIP
FLAPJACKS. I USE A LOT OF HYPERBOLE
AND SNARK. THEY SHOULD HAVE WARNED
YOU.
ARR: THEY DID, KIND OF. THEY SAID THAT
YOU'RE A BIT... OF AN ASS.
ARD: ONLY A BIT? HUH. MUST BE LOSING
MY TOUCH.
ARR: SIGH.
ARD: DID YOU ACTUALLY SIGH THE WORD
SIGH?
ARR: JUST... CONTINUE.

1883 rolls around like it always does, and Doctors Harold Cattell and Allen Olson came to Gravenfrost. They were going to turn the now predominantly headstone island into the perfect spot for an insane asylum. Graves were leveled, roads were paved, and the Gravenfrost Asylum was erected with dilapidated Fort Beacon as their foundation. Something new from something old. Since they were on a roll, they commissioned a modest tuberculosis sanitarium to be attached. Homes were built for staff and physicians, and now America had a nice little place to send their wretched. Out of mind, out of sight. Industry caught wind that there was seaport real estate for the taking, and swooped in with a few factories and shipyards. Now more people came to live on top of the dead. The dark history faded into campfire stories and terrible pillow talk.

ARD: BUT THA GROUND NEVA FORGETS...
AND THA GROUND NEVA FORGIVES.
ARR: WHAT WAS THAT SUPPOSED TO BE?

ARD: THAT'S MY IMPRESSION OF HOW FRED GWYNNE'S CHARACTER IN PET CEMETERY WOULD SAY IT. TELL ME YOU'VE SEEN THAT MOVIE.
ARR: I DON'T CARE FOR HORROR MOVIES, AGENT DOYLE.
ARD: YOU ARE MISSING OUT, LEMME TELL YOU.
ARR: CAN WE PROCEED, PLEASE? INDUSTRY COMES TO GRAVENFROST? THOUGH WHAT THIS HAS TO DO WITH THE CASE IS BEYOND ME.

Fine.

Everyone was happy setting up shop there due to the overlooked cut-corners that nobody would ever bother to investigate. Despite harsh winters and occasional episodes of what the papers called "mass hysteria," things on that cursed floating turd were working out. The 1920s pop up, and a prominent psychiatrist by the name of Oswald Dickinson came to town and started making history. They say that ol' Ozzy had a reputation for using unorthodox and extreme methods of treating the patients at the Asylum. But, he brought the shiny promise of groundbreaking procedures that were going to put the place on the map, so the powers that be saw nothing but dollar signs and headlines. Gravenfrost Asylum and Dickinson went together like beer goggles and bad decisions. It wasn't long before he was made head of his own research department in experimental treatments, and given carte blanche to do whatever his Hammer Horror brain meats could dream up. So, what did he do?

He built a house.
People have been dying in it ever since.

I didn't know all the details heading up to New England, but I knew—hell, anyone who's ever read a ghost story book knew—that the place dubbed "The Devil's Domicile" was bad news bears. The facts get blurry at times, as they often give way to flashlight-in-the-face embellishments, but one story in particular stood out. It's even on file here in the Bureau—The Travers Travesty. In 1975 (because the '70s were the creepiest decade as far as murderous kooks and devil-worshiping shit birds go) a twisted stray pube named Lincoln Travers came to GF, in order to ply his trade in a new territory. His trade: Serial Killing. His M.O.: A little thing called murder-rape, or, "dick-n-die." Not that you need the gritty details, but basically, Travers would kill his victim in the midst of forced intercourse. It wasn't always rape, though. Travers was a handsome guy, and rarely had difficulty coaxing drunken ladies and gentlemen to his bed. Several prostitutes have gone missing along the way as well.

> Wham-bam-shank-you-ma'am.
> I just made that up.
> That'd make a hell of a headline.

Travers managed to convince the Asylum mucky-mucks to hire him as caretaker to the then-rundown Dickinson place. They figured, why not? Maybe the guy'll fix the place up and help show people that it really was just a house after all. Boy-howdy did they screw the pooch on that one. Ol' Dick-n-Die had himself an epiphany soon after moving in: start a cult—a full-fledged, muted color, hair on the camera lens, hush-yo-mouth 1970s cult. You ever watch '70s porn? Like watching Magnum P.I. trying to eat an angry muskrat.

See what happens to the narrative when you don't let me smoke?

People were jumping into the Kool Aid kiddie

pool a lot back then. It didn't take long for the house to
fill up with drug-addled, over-sexed malcontents, who
just wanted to be part of something. Dickhead had it
made. It was a smorgasbord of sweet meat and funky
cheese. He dubbed two of his most devoted followers his
"hands," and they would cherry-pick members for what
they called The Ascension. The lucky duck was bathed
and brought to Travers, who then did his thing. The
member was never seen again. They'd been "taken to the
next level," was the line they used to keep the sheeple
interested in being next. Imagine that—one day you're
on the run, state to state, living off whatever money your
victims had on them, and now you have room-service.

Anyway, blah, blah, blah. Some woman named
Sarah Beck got hip to the jive and escaped. Stuff
occurred, as stuff tends to do, and the POPO organized
an old fashioned stand-off. Travers used his mojo for
one last power play, and had a giant orgy. He knew the
fuzz was going to shut his shit show down, but they
weren't going to stop him from his greatest work, by
golly! He and his two hands, a male and a female,
moved throughout the house while babbling idiotic
pseudo-religious horseshit, and systematically slit the
throats of his followers as they screwed their brains out.
Nobody put up a fight. It was a bloody, drug-fueled,
fuck-frenzy.

When the GFPD and the FBI—who'd been
trying to find this guy for years, yay us!—crashed the
party, only three of the thirty-six cultists were alive.
Travers and his two henchmen. They stood in the grand
foyer, naked and covered in blood. Travers held the
female like a shield, like any true piece of crap would,
and asked the lawmen if they wanted to see true
devotion. The male hench rushed them with a butcher's
knife and a rage boner and got shot to hell. Travers

carved the female cooch-to-tooth, straight up, while she sang "Gimme Shelter" by The Rolling Stones. Her innies became outies as she gurgled the notes. They should have wasted Travers right then and there, but they wanted to take him alive. Nothing like a media frenzy over capturing a serial killer to boost public relations. Travers fought like a beast—even tried to stab himself, but the cops beat him down and locked him away. After the trial, interviews and evaluations, he was deemed clinically insane in the membrane, and sent to the Gravenfrost Asylum to rot. He told the world that the house gave him the idea—that it spoke to him. That meant he was too nutty to fry.

The house made him do it.
Which brings us to the subject of our little interrogation.
Debriefing.
Whatever.

The Devil's Domicile became one of the top five haunted sites to visit. It was widely-known in paranormal circles. Goth kids and murder junkies flocked there to try and catch a glimpse of Dickinson, or a ghost orgy, or whatever it is Goth kids snap their carrots to. Paranormal investigators came in droves as well, thinking the house would be a home run for proof. Cue the muscle-bound ignoramus host of *Spook Show*, filming the Halloween episode. His name is Zane Bagley, and he had reputation for being a bit of a dick. Him and his two stooges, Ned and Andrew, like to bully the ghosts wherever they go. "I'm gonna choke you, ghost!" is his tag line. He was found running through downtown GF, naked as a jaybird, and screaming "Gonna get me, gonna get me!"

It was that thought that warmed me as I crossed

over Procession Bridge in the company SUV, because
you all felt my '69 Charger wasn't Agency enough.
Buildings sat like charcoal mausoleums against the shale
September sky.

Welcome to Gravenfrost Maine.
Population: 3,297 and dropping.
Population below ground: Don't ask.
Try the chowdah.

My partner, Bukowski, let out a little growl to
tell me he was nonplussed. That's right, you people
wouldn't give me a new partner (since Chinatown) so I
brought my shepherd/retriever/mongrel along for the
ride. He likes bacon and licking his balls.

Who doesn't, right?

Downtown looked a lot like every other New
England main drag, for the most part. Murkier, though,
like a watercolor painting that bled into itself. Rows of
stores and cafés, a liquor store with neon words flashing
in the window. The center of town had its post office and
church, and a load of antique shops. There was even the
quintessential town store, complete with crusty old coots
out front playing checkers, smoking pipes, and mean-
mugging me as I passed. Eyes like pin pricks in a thicket
of bushy eyebrows, and mouths trapped in a Whitman
wet dream. I got it—I was the outsider.

Light your torches and grab your pitchforks.

Across the street from the market was a bar
called Last Call, Last Rites. Next to that, Sinclair's
movie house, where a Lucio Fulci marathon was
ransom-noted on the marquee. They only had *one*
Starbucks, which came as a shock. There's no escaping

9

that kind of evil, but they seemed to have held it back some. Good for them. I pulled into the police/fire station next to the market and parked next to a Winnebago. I opened Buk's door, and he sat there like a dope, refusing to heed my various requests that he hop out and take a piss. I lowered his window and shut the door. He'd jump out if he needed.

The GFPD station was quiet, even by Mayberry standards. An Annie Potts-type lady was at a large wooden desk, and spoke to someone named Dustin on her fancy-dancy headset. Dustin was a shitheel, it seemed, by the way she was talking to him. I half expected her to hurry off the line as I approached, maybe pretend that she wasn't tying up an emergency line. But, no, she was too busy tearing Dustin a new poop flume to care. She threw a hold on a minute index finger in the air.

"Listen to me, Dustin!" she shouted. Her voice was like a blend of Cindy Lauper and Herman Munster. "You can't talk your way out of this one! No! You can't! Tammy has her period, and you magically come home with dried *marinara sauce* on your goatee and you expect me to not get suspicious? You don't even like Italian!"

"Excuse me, I—" She shut me down by raising her finger higher. So I stood there like an idiot for what felt like hours, until she slammed her hand on the desk.

"How *dare* you! My Georgia O'Keeffe is beautiful! So? You named your dick Lord of The Minge —I can call my genitals whatever I want! And nice try, trying to change the subject! I don't want you anywhere near me, mister! You hear? You come near me and I'll light you on fire!" She pressed the button on the side of the headset and stabbed me with pale brown eyes.

"Can I help you?"

"I need help."

"What seems to be the problem, sir?"

"My girlfriend's Georgia O'Keeffe looks more like a Jackson Pollock. Do you think she should get that looked at?"

"Sir, I'm going to ask you to leave before I have the Sheriff arrest you for being an asshole." She pushed her glasses up the bridge of her nose and raised a *your move now, bitch* eyebrow. The door behind her opened, and a portly man in his fifties with a badass handlebar 'stache walked through. He shimmied his brown denim jacket on, but struggled to zip it over the basketball he called a gut. He didn't have a cigar or a cowboy hat. That disappointed me greatly.

"Angie, you got any—?" When he saw the sexy bastard in the black suit with impeccable hair, he paused. "What've we got here?"

"Some asshole, Sheriff Laidlaw."

"So you're the fella in charge!" I stepped around the desk and produced my badge and ID. His eyes squinted as he read it. I shot Angie a cocky wink which made her day suck that much more. "I should have known you were the boss, with a cookie duster like that."

"Ah..." he said, like he just realized the show he was watching was a repeat. "You must be Agent Doyle, yeah?"

"That's right, Sheriff. I'm here to—"

"—Take credit from us poor, incapable local folks."

"Well, I was under the impression that you had stumps to jump and sister-aunts to make preggers."

"Son, you *do* realize that we're in the Northeast and not the Deep South, right?"

"That's racist, Sheriff." I smiled. He laughed and shook my hand. Apparently, shit-talking ups your street cred around these parts.

"I'd love to stay and chat, Agent, but it's nearing 1830 hours, and Molly does not tolerate me being late for dinner."

"Right, no reason major homicide can't wait," I said, without holding back the snark.

"No worries, son," Laidlaw chuckled. "My deputy is waiting for you in the back. He's gonna be helping you out with the investigation."

"So this is what Bob Marley was singing about," I mumbled.

"Pardon?"

"What's your deputy's name?"

"He's the only fella back there. You miss him, then the FBI sent the wrong dickhead. G'night, folks!" He waved at Angie and hot-footed it out the door.

"That guy's name is actually Laidlaw? Seems kind of typecast."

"Please go in and see Deputy Walker. I have things to do." Angie snarled her lip.

"Like looking up nice Italian restaurants for Dustin?" I was through the door before she finished gasping.

Deputy Walker was a breath of fresh air. Mid-thirties, tall, ruggedly handsome, and above all? Not a dick. He greeted me with a smile and a strong handshake.

"Agent Doyle, good to meet you. I'm Bruce Walker."

"Likewise, Deputy."

"Bruce. Or Walker, if you prefer."

"Walker it is. Call me Doyle, since we're being chums and all. I'm happy there's at least one person in this town that doesn't treat me like a zombified Jehovah's Witness." We walked over to his desk, and sat.

"You have to understand the small-town dynamic," he smiled. "Outsiders come in, raise hell, and dredge up all the shit we've been trying to forget."

"The Domicile."

"Exactly. Locals know not to screw around there. It's everyone else that thinks it'd be spooky fun to sneak around an abandoned hellhole like that."

"Why not have it demolished?"

"Believe me, I wish we could, but it's on the historical registry. Nobody can touch it unless they plan to restore it. That fucking place should have crumbled into the ground. I'm sure it'll stand for another hundred goddamned years." Irritation and sadness swept across Walker's face, and left as quickly as it came. He reached down and produced a messenger bag from under the desk, and pushed it towards me.

"For you."

"A purse?"

"No. Why does everyone call it that? It's a satchel!"

"So it's a man-bag. Goodie. What's in it?"

"Copies of all the evidence collected at the scene. Footage, photos, the whole shebang."

"Footage, huh? There's got to be a lot of it."

"It's been edited down by... our guy. It shows everything that happened without having to stare at an empty room for hours."

"That's called tampering."

"It's been sanctioned by Sheriff Laidlaw."

"Bully for him. It's still tampering. Look, it's been a long drive, and I could use some grub. I get dicky when I'm hungry."

"I understand. Look, there's an unedited copy in there too. I was about to mention it. Go grab some food. We can meet at the Asylum tomorrow morning around 9 a.m., if that works."

"Sounds like a plan."

"You got a place to stay?"

"Yeah, the Agency set me up at the Sayonara

Motel."

"They must hate you," Walker laughed.

"You have no idea." I stood and we shook hands. "The Last Call joint have good burgers?"

"Great burgers. But you get more for your money at the diner."

"Diners are for transients and the elderly, Walker." I said, as I walked to the door leading to the lobby. "You really want to see the soul of a town, you go to the pub. See you at nine, Deputy."

"Do yourself a solid—you plan to watch that footage tonight? Leave the lights on."

"Don't worry, I brought an extra pair of panties."

*

A man about five-foot-who cares, leaned on the SUV and handed pieces of a Slim Jim to my turncoat dog. He had blond, windswept—possibly overslept—hair, round Ben Franklin glasses and a face that refused to lose its innocence, despite years of knowing better. He also wore a brown trench coat—who the hell wears those anymore? He stood up and smiled as I approached.

"Your dog's a fan of jerky," he said. His voice was deeper than I would have thought, with a sandy quality to it. Not exactly movie trailer narrator, but close.

"That isn't jerky," I grunted as I lit a cigarette. "Jerky comes in strips or chunks, not tubes."

"The real stuff is expensive," he grinned. "I'm Parker Powell." He karate-chopped his hand out for me to shake. I ignored it, because I'm too cool for that.

"The reporter. I've heard of you. You've been on the run ever since you wrote that exposé on that Philly mob boss whatsisname, calling him a pedophile. The Feds found all kinds of horrible shit on his hard drive. The hell was his name?"

"Mal Sal L'Brano. Yeah, I sent him to prison and have been on the run ever since."

"Better than a bullet to the dome, I guess. Wasn't Sal iced in the joint, though?"

"Yeah. You know how the inmates treat pedos. And apparently the Mob disowns you for the same. So Sally had no protection whatsoever."

"Then why are you still running?"

"His son, Alberto, thinks I planted the evidence."

"Mal Al L'Brano. And why would he think that?"

"Because I did!" Parker laughed. He was a strange dude. I liked him immediately, not that I'd let on. "It was easy, really. Sal frequented a lot of porno sites, it didn't take much to hack into his drive from there."

"But that meant you had access to kiddie porn."

"Nope! I was able to use a donor drive for the transfusion. This bastard named Westing was a convicted pedophile that had been released after 'rehabilitation.' The sick shit didn't miss a beat once he was released. He stopped trying to grab kids, and settled on just looking. Rehab for a pedophile should be a bullet, not group sessions. I created a series of mock email conversations between L'Brano and Westing, then dropped a dime."

"Two turds, one flush," I said. Parker smiled.

"Another day at the office."

"Most interesting part of this little back-and-forth is why we're actually having it. What's your angle, Mr. Powell?" His smile grew.

"I know why you're here, Agent Doyle. I know why they sent *you* above all other agents. You're the guy who handles the strange shit. You're the oddball, and you've made a name for yourself in certain circles. We can help each other out."

"That why you told me your dirty little secret?

To scare me with your web-fu? If I don't tell you what I know, you'll zap my hard drive with pictures of my head poorly photo-shopped onto large women's bodies while they bathe in Crisco and breadcrumbs?"

"No... *what*? I told you all that so you would trust me! Now you know a damning secret of mine. I trust you to do the right thing, and I can help you. What you have in that purse—"

"—Satchel... apparently."

"—is only from the most *recent* occurrence." Parker removed a plastic accordion file from his coat. "This is the rest of the Dickinson conspiracy."

"Conspiracy, huh?"

"That's right. Did you know that Dickinson used asylum inmates to build his house?"

"...No."

"His whole thing was the existence of evil. Is it an entity or just something that mankind created? Could it be harnessed? Focused? Absorbed? He took the most violent and psychotic inmates, and somehow got them to build his goddamned house. Every brick, nail, and fleck of paint was touched by the nuttiest of motherfuckers. And the best part?"

"Okay?"

"Not a single one of them survived the construction. They say Dickinson buried them in the mortar and foundation."

"That sounds like local color to me. Listen, Mr. Powell, I'm not here to put any souls to rest, or dick-punch the devil. I'm here for a TV host that went tuxedo collar-popping crazy, and fled a house full of his dead buddies. I'm not going to concern myself with ghost stories."

"It's all connected. I want to expose it. I want to end it."

"As long as you stay the hell out of my way, I'm not going to stop you. Now if you don't mind, I'd like to go eat. It was nice meeting you. Best of luck with the mob." I waved his folder off and got in the SUV. It would have been a decent scene ending if the stupid bar wasn't located across the street. Ah, well. I could have headed to the diner across town, but I needed a beer. Besides, a diner is the heart of a town—what I needed was its guilty conscience.

2

A DOG AND A JACKASS WALK INTO A BAR...

The first thing that hit me as I entered the Last Call, Last Rites bar and grille, was the scent of old wood and salt air. Like the Gorton's Fisherman cracked out a hard fart. To the left of the door was the pool table/darts/bathrooms, to the right were the tables and booths. Straight ahead the wall-length bar stood like a row of unpolished coffins. People huddled in small clutches around the tables and stuffed booths—eyeballing me. There was an eerie quiet to the place.

Reverent.
Conversations were just whispers in beer mugs.

"You can't bring *that* dog in here," the hostess said. She wasn't a day over nineteen, but looked like she could hold her own. She was one of those tough, hot New England girls you hear about.
"Well, what dog *can* I bring in, then?" I shrugged. Bukowski tilted his like, *who, me*?

"None?"

"He's my designated driver." I smiled. She stared at me and huffed.

"Fiiine. Take that booth over there... your server will be right wiiith you." She walked back to the bar and took a shot of what looked like vodka. Buk and I sat and I perused the laminated sheet menu. The hostess took a deep breath, muttered to herself and walked back over. "Hi, I'm Jenny. What can I get you?"

"Hi, Jenny, I'd like a flagon of your finest grog and a bowl of water for my colleague."

"A faggot of what?"

"Never mind. Whatever local lager you have, a grilled chicken breast with sweet potato fries, and a Beacon bacon burger. No onions. Any burger named after Fort Beacon must be good, right?"

"Waffle fries?"

"Waffle fries."

"How do you want the burger cooked?"

"Medium well. Just enough juice to know it was alive, and grizzled enough to know it's not a zombie."

"You're weird."

"Yeah." I smiled and she walked toward the kitchen. I took the opportunity to slide out of the booth and mosey over to the jukebox. One quarter, one song. My coin went clunk, and after a few button pushes, the low murmurs turned into "The Man in Black" by Johnny Cash. A few of the old-timers nodded as I walked back to the booth. To my delight, my beer was waiting for me, and Buk was already lapping at his water. There was something else there, too. The damn accordion folder.

Fucking journalists.

'There's so much more to this' was scribbled on a sticky-note stuck to the folder. A cell phone number was scratched below it with the last few drops of ink in the

pen. I didn't even start this investigation, and I've already been tossed a bucket of conspiracy theories by a screwball that lives in a Winnebago. Don't get me wrong, Powell's done some Grade-A super sleuthing, but this caper is the work of a mental breakdown, not a *Scooby Doo* villain. Nine times out of ten, it isn't cursed land or haunted Kewpie dolls, but a dude with an ax and non-functioning circuitry. But it was that remaining one out of ten that convinced me to open the folder. A picture of a buxom blonde with her midsection open like a baked potato slid out just as Jenny started to set the place settings down. She instead dropped them onto the table, causing the fork to clatter to the floor.

"Jesuswhatthefuck?!" she yipped. I hastily shoved the pic back into the folder and set the clasp.

"Yeah, sorry—I—sorry." I chugged the beer as best I could to buy some time.

"What. The. Actual. Fuck. Was that?"

"That? Eh... well? My new special effects artist at work. Heh. You see... I'm a movie producer, and this guy sent me a whole portfolio of his work. Guess if he could get that kind of reaction from you, I should probably hire him on the spot, right?"

"That was wicked brutal, dude!" Jenny's eyes lit up. "You should totally hire him! So... a producer, huh?" she bit her lower lip seductively.

"Yes. I produce obscure indie flicks." The bullshit floweth.

"Anything I've ever seen?"

"My latest was *It Takes Ten to Tango in the Park of Our Encumbrance.*"

"Never heard of it. What's it about?"

"Haaa, well, my dear, it's not something you can explain. It's only something you can experience."

"I get you. So... you looking to fill any other roles?" Jenny leaned on the table, and twirled her ponytail.

"Matter of fact, I am." I winked. Her smile nearly split her head in two. "I'm looking for a girl who looks just you to fill a small, but very important role."

"OH EM GEE! Tell me, tell me!"

"She takes a glass like this one." I held up my glass.

"Yeah? AND?"

"She gets me more beer."

3
A TOMB WITH A VIEW

I'm a dick.

I'm sure that was established ages ago, but I feel the need to just put it out there. I felt a twinge of guilt for leading the waitress on the way I did. But I can't help it, sometimes. Maybe it's a defense mechanism or maybe Mom bounced me off the kitchen floor a few times. Who knows? Either way. I'm a dick. That was my mantra as I drove from the bar to the Sayonara Motel, the crap factory where *you guys* set me up. It overlooked one of the prominent cemeteries, which was a very quaint touch. Really, kudos all around.

The main office was small and looked like Ed Wood shat all over it. Pictures from just about every horror movie covered the walls and every flat surface. There was even a small section dedicated to famous people who have stayed there. It was blank, except for a picture of Godzilla. The greasy matchstick in a blue and gray bowling shirt behind the counter was the owner, Mack. He sat on a high stool and read a copy of *Science*

Friction.

You know what that is, Agent Remender? No? It's a skin mag that features a lot—a LOT—of costumes and Cosplay. You know, like pictures of a dude dressed as Doctor Who taking Sailor Moon to pound-town.

Not that I've ever read it.
Anyway.

I stood at the counter for a full minute, watching *Plan 9 From Outer Space* on the crappy little TV that sat on a stack of magazines. I smacked the service bell that let out a sickly *donk*, which caused the toothpick between Mack's salted-slug lips to stop swirling.

"You see me sittin' here, right?" Mack said, with a voice that I can only describe as Tom Waits on helium.
"You see me *standing* here, right?" I nodded.
"I was focusin' on my literature, as a matter of fact." He set his prose down and gave me the once over. "You must the fed. Your bosses set you up in our most famous and special room, you know that?"
"I'm so loved. Tell me, what amazing room did they book for me?"
"The Su Room."
"Like... Peggy Sue?"
"Like suicide," Mack chuckled. "Folks are always offin' themselves in that room. Maybe it's due to the location of the motel, particularly the Su Room, in the vortex between the asylum and the Domicile."
"The *vortex*?"
"Yeah, you know, that room is practically dead center between them. Also, being so close to the graveyard, I'm sure there's all kinds'a energy seriously finger-blastin' that room. And *that's* the room they chose for you, you lucky guy! They must really care."

23

"Yeah, we get along like dirigibles and fire."

"Well, let me ask you one question before I hand the room keys over."

"Okay."

"Have you seen 'em with your own eyes?"

"Who?"

"The aliens, man! You're *X-Files* all up in your ass!"

"I'm not sure that's an actual sentence."

"Have you SEEN 'em?" his eyes got wide and glazed.

"You want the scoop from the ice cream man, you have to give him something in return."

"Name it."

"You got any hooch?"

"Do I look like a drinker to you?"

"Absolutely."

"Well, you're right. What do you want? I have a bunch of stuff in the back. Usually, it's whatever is left behind by the people in the Su Room. Heheh. Name your poison."

"Whiskey."

"Oh, I have just the thing!" Mack disappeared to the back room behind a red curtain, and returned with a bottle with a skull on the label. "This here, my friend, is called Graves End whiskey. Made right here in Gravenfrost!"

"This crap-shack town actually has a distillery?" I was impressed *and* slightly worried. If it's local, they use local water. Water taken from ground that's saturated by the dead. Worry quickly turned to thirst as Mack handed the bottle over. It was pretty. The skull had a handlebar mustache. The tag-line was, *"Our spirits are out to get you."* Adorable.

"Now, dish on the aliens, Agent man!"

"Alright. Since you gave me an unopened bottle, I'll give you the straight dope: Aliens are real and have been living among us forever. Most of the people you know are shape-shifting spacemen."

"Like who?"

"Tom Cruise's hair dresser, Adrien Brody, Whoopi Goldberg, and Bono. There's a lot more, but—"

"Martha Stewart?"

"Ol' Martha's a class ten demigod." I smiled as I plucked the keys from his hand.

"I fuckin' knew it!" Mack shouted and slammed his fist. "You have a good night, man. I gotta go update my blog!" I took my leave and drove the truck down the row of identical red doors till I was at the Su Room. The cemetery on the other side of the fence was impressive, even in the dark. Twisted trees, crumbling stone walls that barely kept the hilly stone-marked expanse at bay.

The Su Room wasn't lacking in the *what the hell did I get myself into now?* department either. If ridiculous was a category in Better Homes and Mausoleums, this crap hole would win the golden mailbox award. The walls and carpet were a deep burgundy, and dozens of oddly-sized paintings and photos hung slapdash around the joint. Bukowski darted in and hopped on the bed nearest the radiator. He plopped himself down like he had such a hard day at work. I set my suitcase down and tossed the satchel and folder on the other bed and wondered just what the buttery fuck the deal was.

I removed the painting of a '20s-era woman walking a cheetah on a leash above the headboard of my bed, revealing a crappily-spackled wall. The paint was so cheap I could still make out the divots that used to be buckshot, and discoloration that used to be brain-splatter patterns. I looked up at the nub in the ceiling that was once a fan, now capped off because Mack was either too tired of cutting people down or too cheap to keep replacing damaged fans. Over the nightstand was a photo of Sammy Hagar, of all people, which covered what looked like a crossbow bolt hole. Bolt hole. That's fun to say. Sweet baby Elvis, that room was freak-city. I didn't even want to see the condition of the bath tub. If Mack didn't bother covering up medieval-themed suicides properly, I could only imagine he'd leave one hell of a ring around the tub from all those Susies.

Susies.
That's my new tag for people who do themselves in.
Spread the word, okay?

I sat against the headboard and removed the cork to the whiskey. It had an earthy scent, like the woods after a good rain, and the taste? It was like somebody set autumn on fire—woody, smoky and surprisingly smooth. It reminded me of when I was a dick Goth teenager taking pictures in graveyards at night with chicks that only saw me as a friend. Anyway... damn tasty whiskey.

What? Are you pissed that I just admitted to drinking on the job, or that I tried to be Goth? Yes, so I drank. Twice in one night. Gerald in Archives smokes crack—none of us are role models, sweetheart.

I dumped the contents of the satchel onto the bed, and spread them out. Crime scene photos to the left, written statements to the right. But what I was really interested in was the footage. I fired up my laptop and inserted the disc titled "Spook Show: Devil's Domicile," and took another swig. I plugged in my headphones when I heard the guy in the next room sound like he was eating kielbasa without chewing. At least I didn't have to hear the majestic sounds of humping coming from my

26

other neighbors in the graveyard. Then again, who knew in that crazy-ass town?

First thing we see is the show's three hosts standing at the iron gate to the Dickinson property, looking like they're trying to not shit themselves. It was late afternoon by the look of it. Their leader—muscle and hair gel aficionado—and our only witness, Zane Bagley, flexed his chest and smiled like the douche he is.

"Hello, I'm Zane Bagley, and welcome to another *Spook Show* adventure! Tonight, The Spook Crew and I are embarking on what could be our most dangerous investigation yet! That's right! On the other side of this gate lies the infamous Dickinson Estate, better known as The Devil's Domicile! Dozens of gruesome murders and deaths have occurred here, and it's slated as one of the scariest haunting locations in the world! Some fucked up shit, yo!" The three idiots laughed. "We can edit that out." Zane flexed again.

"Okay, let's get the local guy in the frame," the cameraman said. "Chuck?" A short, portly fellow with an amateur beard and a shirt that said *Han Fired First* approached the hosts and smiled awkwardly at the camera, like he farted at a job interview.

"With us is local Gravenfrost paranormal expert, Chuck Gibblin." Zane flexed. "Thanks for coming out."

"*Hehhnn...* Th-thanks for—happy to," Chuck was visibly jittery.

"Let's try that again," Zane smiled. "We're about to lose daylight, and we need to set up the static cameras."

"Right, s-sorry, Zane," Chuck stammered. "Glad to be here, Zane! Happy to help the Spook Crew get to the bottom of The Devil's Domicile! *Hehhnn...*"

"What can you tell me about this place, Chuck?"
"Well..."

Blah.
Blah.
Blah.

Fast forward through a ton of flexing and nut scratches until they entered the gate. Close up on Zane's face as he tries to look as tough as possible with such a dopey haircut.

"Okay, we're about to enter one of the most hauntedest places on the world."

Really, Zane? Hauntedest on the world?

Suddenly, Zane's face shot up. The camera spun back toward the sidewalk, where Chuck had taken off like a striped-ass baboon. "Where the hell are you going?" Zane shouted after Chuck. The camera spun back toward the Queen Anne-style mansion. A figure in the second story window darted from view.

"Holy shit!" the camera guy bleated.

"You get that, Steve? *Please* tell me you got that!"

"Shit yeah! Yeah, I got it, man! Looked like a chick!"

"Looked like a shadow to me," Andrew offered. Zane did a little freaky hop-flex thing.

"Chuck got scared off like a little fag! Let's get in there and start making history, people! Tell the others to get the rest of the crap out of the van." Andrew did as Zane ordered, and walked to their van.

"You think we might actually catch something we didn't set up?" Ned rubbed his hands together.

"Shut *up*, Ned!" Zane punched his chubby pal in the shoulder. "Steve, close up on me. Let's find out *who* or *what* that was! That's going in the commercial." Zane

28

pulled at his black t-shirt with shiny silver skulls on it, and popped his neck. The footage jumped to Andrew's hand-held camera sweeping the grand foyer—a large rotunda with a winding staircase to the right, that led up to the second floor, which wrapped around the open space with two long-ass hallways to either side. A skinny blonde with ripped jeans and one of those hippie wool caps stood in the middle of the rotunda and shivered.

"This is the spot where the Travers showdown took place!" she said excitedly.

"Tara, set up a static camera facing that spot, maybe a FLIR, too. We should try some EVPs if the acoustics aren't shit." Andrew panned toward the sitting room to the right of the front door. Ned, another male, and two female crew members were rummaging through the bric-a-brac.

"Andy, check this out," Ned waved him over. "There's still crap here—books and junk. I'm surprised it hasn't been looted. And look!" Ned turned the switch to a desk lamp, which snapped to life with a dust-covered, dehydrated piss yellow glow.

"Why is there electricity?"

"This place is on the historical registry, right?" The girl with the purple hair and nose ring shrugged, while examining a torn book about birds of prey. "Maybe someone's been trying to restore it."

"We needed permission from the hospital to film here, right? Andrew said. "Guess it doesn't matter. Let's get finished setting—"

BOOM!

A loud crash came from the second floor. Shaky camera to the foyer, followed by several *omigod!*'s then Zane and Steve leaning on the balcony railing, laughing.

"Sorry! I knocked a lamp over." Zane chuckled.

"Me and Steve didn't see any shadow woman. Just a bunch of weird fucking rooms. We're all set up, though. You guys hit the basement yet?"

"Not yet, Z," Andrew scratched his goatee. "There's electricity, though! We can use the outlets instead of the batteries."

"Yeah, me and Steve figured it out, like, an hour ago." Zane flexed. Steve rolled his eyes. "Ned, take Brenda and set up the basement. It's dark out, and we need to start."

"Whatever... I'm going outside for a smoke." Brenda Purplehairington grunted as she zipped up her Bullet for My Valentine hoodie. She tugged and pushed against the front door, but it wouldn't give. "What the hell? Who locked the door?"

"Doors lock from the inside. Maybe your chubby fingers are too greasy?" Zane smirked.

"Eat me, roid bitch."

"Fat free meals for me, sorry." What a shit taco.

"Asshole," Brenda lit her cigarette and puffed with a vengeance. "Let's go, Ned." They walked toward the kitchen, where the cellar door was. Andrew's camera panned to Tara in the rotunda. She set up the camcorder on a tripod while singing to herself.

I knew that song.
"Gimme Shelter."

Either Tara read the same Wikipedia page I did, or she was getting psychic impressions without even knowing it. The footage switched to Steve's camera. He was focusing on Zane, while keeping the dark hallway in view. A shape formed in the grainy bullshit darkness. For a shadow person, it had great hips.

"Holy tits!" Steve shouted. Zane spun around and saw the shape sink back into the murk.

"Go! Get it!" Zane howled and ran into the

30

hallway with Steve on his heels. "Hey! Get back here! I'm gonna choke you, ghost!" The flashlights on their cameras cut at the darkness like an epileptic carving a turkey. They barely made it halfway down the corridor before they realized the shape they were chasing was gone. Andrew panted as he caught up to his buddies.

"Wha-What did—*pant*—you guys see?"

"Get the camera on me." Zane rolled his shoulders. Andrew obliged. "We just chased a shadow person down this hallway. We must have scared him off, though. He's gone."

"Looked like a woman to me," Steve said.

"Whatever. At least we got it on tape, right?" He turned the knob to the nearest room and poked the hand held in. "Let's split up and check these rooms."

"Split this!" Steve protested while grabbing his crotch off camera (I assume). "We should regroup with Ned and the girls, not pull some horror movie bullshit!"

"You *scared*, man?" Zane got in real close.

"Shit yeah! What we just saw was—"

"Our ticket to fame and fortune. You wanna be a pussy? Fine. Be a pussy and fuck off back to Pittsburgh. You want to be a part of history? Nut up and pick a fucking room."

"Okay, okay, shit!" Steve hung the camera low as he composed himself.

"Andrew, take this room and do some EVPs." Zane ordered. Andrew nodded and stepped in. Zane closed the door behind him.

Andrew felt the wall for a light switch and flipped it up. A single bulb in the middle of the room buzzed. He turned the camera on himself and rubbed his lips.

"This is Andrew... second floor of the Dickinson House. I'm standing in a room painted completely black.

I'm gonna try to get an EVP, or, Electronic Voice Phenomenon, with my digital recorder." He slid the recorder out of his black utility vest and pressed record. "I feel, like, electricity in the air. Thick. The hair on my neck and arms are standing up. You know what? I'm going to use another device while recording—my ovilus. The spirits can use this to communicate directly. Hold on..." he set his backpack down and rummaged through until he removed what looked like a graphing calculator. He turned it on and it let out a light, static sound.

"Is there anybody—"

Hidden, the ovilus stated in a creepy robot voice.

"H-Hidden?" Andrew stammered. "That was fast! What's hidden?"

Black.

Light.

"Black light. What do you…?"

Show.

Light.

Hidden.

"The hell? This thing usually just spouts out bullshit algorithm words. Black. Light. The room is black—is the light bothering you?" Then it hit him. "Oh, wait!" He reached back into his bag and pulled out a small black light used for crime scene investigations.

Yes, the ovilus stated. Andrew slapped the room light off and fired up the black light.

Ting ting ting, the black light flashed on. The entire room ignited in an iridescent torrent of bright green and white designs—circles within circles within triangles, scripted with demonic-looking words, which caused Andrew to convulse and drop his equipment. His camera swayed like a pendulum on his wrist lanyard. The footage immediately cut to the static night vision camera in the far corner. Whoever edited this stuff should get an Emmy. Andrew stood at the epicenter of fourteen converging diagrams like he was being electrocuted. The black light shattered, but the designs remained.

After thirty seconds or so of intense freak-out, Andrew slumped like a lumbering beast. His breathing was heavy and laced with deep growls. He flung the door open with a deafening slam, and tore ass toward the balcony overlooking the foyer. Tara and the other female (file said her name was Sydney) were talking to Phil by the front door. Phil looked like a hipster who "dabbles" in politics. You know the kind, facial hair and converse knockoffs, saying how nobody should ever speak against his first amendment rights, while in the same breath telling you to keep your rightist opinion to yourself even though you aren't left or right, but felt the need to insert some logic into his crap argument about how hugs and kale deter crime.

What was I saying?

Oh, right. So, Andrew leaned over the railing and laughed with what sounded like eight voices. Tara looked up and gasped.

"Andy! Your eyes are bleeding!" She screamed. Phil and Sydney rushed up the stairs. Phil turned Andrew around to get a better look.
"Dude! You look like shit! We need to get you to a hospital!"
"The hell happened?" Zane and Steve down the hallway toward the fracas. Andrew turned to Zane and smiled, then spun quicker than the camera could catch, and bit Phil in the throat.

Everybody froze.

Andrew tore a massive Hamburger Helper hole

in Phil's neck, then pitched him over the balcony rail. The sound of his skull hitting the terrazzo floor was a mix between a shattering coffee mug, a heavy bag being punched, and spaghetti being rapidly stirred in a pot. Andrew turned back to Zane and lunged. Zane pushed Steve toward him and ran. Andrew lifted Steve up by the throat several feet off the floor. Tara railed against the front door, which still refused to open. Sydney stood silent, in shock. Andrew took hold of Steve's leg with his free hand and released his throat. Andrew dragged him to the black light room, where the symbols got so bright that the static camera began to fritz, then blacked out. The audio still worked, though, as Steve's screams turned to maniacal laughter.

I hit pause and lit a cigarette. I looked over at Bukowski, and watched his back leg kick as he slept. I took another pull of Graves End, took a deep breath, and then hit play.

"Gonna GET you! Gonna GET you!" The twisted voice of Andrew sang as he ran from door-to-door, sniffing the air at each stop. His camera swung wildly on his wrist strap, until he finally ripped it off and threw it down the hallway where Steve now dragged Sydney kicking and screaming down the opposite hallway.

"Gonna GET you! Gonna GET you!" Zane heard Andrew's voice trail off, and slowly slid out from under the bed. His camera was set on green-porno night vision, and he turned it toward himself. He had no clue about the woman with half her face missing that stood on the other side of the bed, pointing at him.

"Gotta... conserve battery. Luh-long night." he whispered, then the screen went dark.

*

Flashlights swayed in the nearly abyssal cellar, doing just this side of diddly squat. Ned and Brenda had just finished setting up the static camera on the tripod when they heard the scream.

"The fuck was that?" Ned jumped.

"You know those pussies up there. Probably saw Zane's shriveled dick, and screamed in utter sadness for him."

"He's gonna see this footage, you know."

"Don't care. Hey, look at this!" Brenda took Ned by his sleeve over to an old wooden table covered in all kinds of macabre crap. It looked like an altar. Behind it, the seal of Asmodeus was painted on the wall. As a demonologist, I can tell you he is a *baaaaad* dude, even by Hell's standards.

"Looks like an altar," Brenda stated. I liked Brenda. She's a tad archetypal, but she's got a modicum of smarts. The static night vision camera they set up began to turn to the right, toward the stairs, and another scream was heard.

"We better go and see what's going on." Ned said. As they approached the steps, I heard a rush of feet, then suddenly Brenda was pulled into the dark by what to me looked like two people in black body stockings, but the footage was grainy and green, and really low quality. It was something to note, though. Ned ignored Brenda's begs for help, and ran/tripped up the stairs in a panic. Brenda's shouts turned into the sounds of repetitive cranial trauma by the time Ned made it to the kitchen. He spotted Tara kneeling in the foyer and didn't stop until he nearly slipped on Phil's goopage.

"Holy! Tara! What!" Ned stammered. Tara shuddered as the tears and grief snot fell. She used Ned's limbs to pull herself up.

"We—we—have to-to-to hide!" she choked out the words.

35

"What happened to Phil? Where is everyone?"
Steve and Sydney appeared above them on the landing
and smiled. Sydney let out an ungodly guttural moan.
Her jaw stretched to the point of looking unhinged. Her
eyes were pools of ink. Something sinister was inside
her now, and whatever it was, it looked like it was
having a blast. Andrew appeared, face covered in blood,
and waved at Ned. Tara pulled Ned toward the kitchen
as Steve and Andrew playfully made their way to the
stairs.

"Gonna GET you! *HEEEeeeeEEE!"* Andrew
laughed. Tara and Ned crashed into the walk-in pantry.
Ned grabbed the wooden case that held rotted cookbooks
and pulled it down across the door. Funny, how nobody
ever thinks to put down the camera in these situations.
It's like it becomes their hand. I'd like to think I would
use the camcorder as a bludgeoning apparatus.

Another fun word to say.
Apparatus.

Steve and Andrew raged against the door,
causing it to splinter. It held, though, thanks to the
bookcase. After a small eternity, the pounding stopped.
Ned's hyperventilation was sound enough, though. Tara
set the camera on a metal rack and began rummaging for
food through empty, decomposing boxes and bins.

"What are you doing?"
"Looking for food."
"In an abandoned house? Why would there be
——"

"Because it's a fucking haunted house, I don't
know! Maybe there's something to eat!"
"I'll give you something to eat!" Steve howled
from the other side of the door.
"Shut the *FUCK* up, Steve!" Tara roared.

"*HEEEE!*" Steve laughed. Something happened to the camera then. It buzzed and distorted. Grotesque images and sounds flashed intermittently with images of Tara pacing and twitching and huddling and laughing and crying and screaming at the two goofballs in the kitchen, then twitching some more. Faces appeared around the pantry, and only the camera and Tara could see them. Ned sat against the book shelf, trying to sleep.

"Ned. Ned." Tara whispered.

"Yuh?" Ned roused from what I'm sure was a crappy nap.

"So hungry. How long have we been in here?"

"Watch says it's six."

"A.M.?"

"P.M."

"We've been in here for seventeen hours?! How?!"

"They chased us, we ran. The end."

"How...?" Tara began to convulse. "Shut up shut up shut up!" she screamed.

"I didn't say anything!" Applauding and hooting could be heard from the other side of the door.

"Not you! No! Shut up! Get out!" The camera freaked out again. There was so much chaotic noise going on that I had to mute the computer. Finally, Tara stood stock still.

"You okay?" Ned held out a shaky hand. Tara slowly reached for her camera, and put her face in close. She smiled.

"You got it, Cyrus?" Andrew asked through the door.

"Yeh," Tara replied in a raspy voice.

"What are you—?" Ned's question was cut short by the savage camera-to-face action Tara heaped upon him. The final shot of the room was from inside Ned's face looking up at a bloodied, distorted Tara, who stepped over him. I could hear her lift the shelf and exit the pantry.

"Feels good, don't it?" Andrew said.

"Been a while." Steve sighed.

"Yeh," Tara said. "Let's finish it."

*

The camcorder light accentuated the terror on Zane's face. He looked ragged and ready to crack. The camera's microphone picked up harsh and menacing whispers. Like a movie theater lobby full of psychopaths —voices blending into one indiscernible sound. He was in a room full of dolls, which is never a good thing, regardless of a house being haunted or not.

I never understood the appeal of keeping dolls that look like perfectly-preserved SIDS babies displayed like it's not supposed to creep out your guests. 'Look, this seemingly dead child is wearing a baseball uniform. I ordered him from the Never Have Guests Again catalog.

Precious.

"Gonna get me... gonna get me..." Zane stammered. "Wearing my friends' skin... not my friends. Gonna get me... every room a trap... the voices. The voices. Made my way downstairs. Windows, doors don't work. Eyes and teeth and fingers like kitchen knives. Phones don't work. Gonna get me... gonna try the basement."

Oh... don't do that. That's never a good idea.

"Gonna... gotta..." his head darted up and if he heard something. I raised the volume and wished I didn't. A cacophony of insidious voices were all babbling at once.

> *They want you.*
> *She wants you.*
> *We aaaalll want you.*
> *I want his eyes.*

All the dolls turned their heads.

I jotted *she* on my notepad and took another needed swig of Graves End. By the date on his camera, Zane's been playing hide-and-seek for nearly two days. They entered the house Friday evening, and it was now pushing Sunday. But that didn't add up. You don't hide in a haunted house, especially one of that caliber. Every inch of that place should be sending sonar pings to his pursuers. He should have been dead or turned into one of those freaks out there within the first few hours.

They were breaking him.

A slurry of footfalls ended just outside the door. Zane held his breath. In a fluid motion, Sydney entered the room, closed the door, and pressed her back to it.

"Zane? You're alive?" she panted.

"NO!" Zane screamed and ran to the far wall. His impact caused an avalanche of memento mori on his head.

"SHH! Shut up, they'll hear us!" she whispered. Zane looked like a squirrel in the road trying to figure out what the hell to do as a minivan rushed toward it.

"Didn't get you?" Zane said.

"No! Come with me, I know a safe place!" Oh, Zane, don't do it, man. Reluctantly, he let her take his hand, and together they ran into the hallway. Right into Steve's waiting arms.

"InZane in the membrane!" Steve chuckled.

"Hey! Look who I found!" Steve tightened his bear hug, but Zane's muscles were too big to fully hold. Zane went into full fight-or-flight mode, and drove his forehead into Steve's nose, causing him to lose his grip. Zane jammed his thumbs into Steve's eye sockets with all his strength.

"OOO! Ha! Yes!" Steve howled. The camera in the hallway began to pixelate. "Atta boy, Zaney! Hoo HOO! Get in there! Dig, motherfucker, dig!"

"Shutupshutup!" Zane smashed Steve's head into the wall. Once. Twice. Still, he laughed.

"Here!" Sydney shoved a curved, bone-handle knife at Zane. He took it with his right hand and drove it up between Steve's ribs repeatedly. The laughter stopped. Sydney pulled him away from the body, and led him like a drunk to another room.

"In here." She opened the door and nudged him in. She flicked the light on, and it was unbearable to Zane. It wasn't so great for me either, thanks for asking. The room was the size of a master bedroom, but without furniture. Instead, the walls, ceiling, and floor were covered in ornate mirrors of various sizes. The single bulb light in the ceiling refracted and doubled, quadrupled as it bounced off the mirrors.

"Where?" Zane stammered. Poor guy was at the front desk of the Sanity Inn, about to check out.

"Shhhh, it's alright," Sydney kissed him. "This is where you will be safe." She undressed, and it was pretty awesome, all things considered.

"Wh-what are you doing?" Zane asked. He was still that squirrel.

"Put the camera down, baby," she cooed. Don't put it down, I pleaded. Zane, bless his heart, set it down but kept recording the images in the mirrors. "We want you to be our new Thaumaturgy."

"A whu-what?"

"Our miracle worker. Our magician." She

clutched his crotch. "Would you like to fuck me, Mage?" She kissed him again. "You can do anything you want to me." The knife fell from Zane's trembling hand. She ripped his shirt open, revealing his love of sit-ups. She kissed his neck, his chest, his abs. Somehow, Zane managed to get a full fear-boner, which Sydney took enthusiastic, gobbley advantage of. Zane shook off his jeans as—

Less about that?
You sure? I—okay.

As Sydney (or whoever it was) did their thing, the mirrors started to darken and swirl. Silhouettes formed and stretched the glass like latex gloves as though trying to push their way out. From this angle, something that wasn't saliva started to drip from Sydney's face. Zane opened his eyes and saw the mirrors. As he tried to remove himself, Sydney grabbed his ass and pulled him back in. In that split second, the camera caught a glimpse of what was dripping—*blood*. From her eyes. Make that a lesson, kids, never trust haunted house head. Zane managed to slip free and backpedaled like he was trying to put a Flintstones car in reverse, and ultimately fell on his bare ass. Sydney lunged for him, but he kicked her away, then scrambled to his feet. He ran from the room without his pants. The static foyer camera caught Zane running toward the staircase with Tara standing in the way, arms open wide. Zane had no time to pity no fools, and rammed her at full speed. Somehow, she vaulted backwards over the balcony railing, and added another coat of head juice to the floor below. I rewound those frames and watched it again. A fraction before impact, it looks like Tara jumps toward the railing, allowing Zane's force to send her over.

She wanted to die?

Zane took the stairs in practically one jump, and smashed against the front door. Still, that bastard wouldn't budge. Sydney appeared above and blew him kisses. Zane ran into the kitchen and down the stairs to the basement. He looked around the blackened room, searching for a way out. Mists swirled and orbs flew rapidly around the morbid cellar. Andrew stirred around the side of the stairs.

"HE'S RIGHT THERE!" I shouted. Couldn't help myself. Bukowski raised his head just high enough to give me the stink eye. "Sorry, Buk." I said. He huffed and went back to doggie dream land.

"Gonna GET you!" Andrew shrieked as he rushed to tackle Zane into the altar. Skulls and parchments fell to the floor as they struggled. Zane lifted Andrew and slammed him hard to the concrete floor. Without hesitation, Zane straddled his old friend and began to smash one of the skulls into Andrew's head like a monkey using a rock to open a coconut. Zane screamed for three full minutes, as the skull turned to shards of bone mashed into what was once Andrew's face. The basement light turned on, Zane was surrounded by mutilated visions of the dead—reaching for him. He took off out of camera view, deeper into the basement. The report stated that he found a storm door, and was able to free himself. That was when he was found running down main street, stark naked and stark raving.

Meanwhile... Sydney sat on the balcony railing, kicking her legs. She picked her teeth with the tip of the bone-handle knife.

"He's gone. We failed. What? You suppose it's

that simple? *Yesssss...* closer at least. Thirty Six." She
wrapped her legs between the railings and pulled the
knife across her stomach. Her entrails slopped down like
snakes from a sauce pot. Once the final plop plopped,
her body was counter-balanced on the rail, and she sat
there like a used meat piñata. That's when the shadow
people reappeared from the corners of the camera frame
like they were actively trying to stay out of sight. I
figured out why, too, they reflected light, which made
them as solid as you and me. Which meant they were
most likely alive. A whole new can of worms popped
open. The editor of the film decided to pan through the
cameras, revealing as much carnage as he could possibly
find. Either that, or he was trying to catch the not-so-
shadow people from another angle and failed. The disc
ejected and I closed the laptop. I needed to chew on the
crazy shit I just watched—process it. But even more
importantly?

I needed to pee.

*

After an eternal piss-o-rama, I stepped out into
the murky night and lit a cigarette. It wasn't terribly cold,
but chilly and moist enough to tighten my skin. I felt the
burn of the cool salt air and smoke in my lungs, and
looked toward the graveyard. It's amazing, really—
people will build on just about anything. Take that town
for instance; the island was rejected by the sea, cursed
and hollow. But man buried all that under the weight of
industry and profit. It goes to show you, though—it
doesn't matter if you go to the gym, eat your veggies,
smoke, drink, or go to church. Doesn't matter how many
digits are in your bank account, you're still gonna end up
in the dirt. My father once told me that Grandpa asked to
be cremated and placed in a Savarin Coffee can. When

Dad asked why, Grandpa said, "I like that coffee."
Bukowski trotted out and took a lengthy piss in the
bushes, then trotted back to bed. I stamped out the butt
and did the same.

It was 11:34 p.m., and I knew I had an early day
ahead of me. But the cigs were at war with the booze,
making me tired, but not sleepy. So I figured what the
hell, and opened the file Parker Powell gave me. I
dumped it out—reports, newspaper clippings, and crime-
scene photos bearing his damn sticky-notes. He sure did
love those things. I held up a picture of the newly-built
house with Oswald Dickinson standing in front looking
like Freud's evil twin. The sticky-note said *'flip,'* so I did.
I'm used to taking those orders from my local rub-and-
tug joints.

Don't give me that look.

It said Dickinson started construction in 1922,
using thirty six extremely psychotic and violent inmates,
as some sort of "work therapy." Every one of them died.
There aren't any records of where their bodies were
interred or if they were even removed from the house.
That not only jives with what Parker said, but with the
crazy shit I just watched. Thirty six. What's the
significance? I'd have to look into it when I wasn't so
drun... tired. So darn tired. On the back of the photo was
also a list of the inmates' names, and one practically
screamed at me—Cyrus Walsh—Paranoid
Schizophrenic and child rapist/murderer.

Sonuvabitch.

Next pic was of the house, but with a dapper
family standing out front.1950. Lawyer named Thomas
Len purchased the house, and within a few months, went

"The Shining" on his wife, kids and live-in nanny. The crime-scene photos left little to the imagination as to what an ax can do to a human body. Mrs. Len was the woman in the photo that fell out at the bar, by the way. The baked potato? Parker wrote that the police had been called several times prior to the murder for intruder complaints and domestic disturbances. The nanny said that Mr. Len had been hearing voices throughout the house, and had become more and more aggressive. Police found him hanging from the balcony by his intestines that he managed to wrap around his neck. What is it about intestines?

1956: Horror movie shoot goes completely bonkers as the lead actress spontaneously combusted during an exorcism scene. The male lead was quoted as saying, "It was laughing. I never heard a house laugh before."

The 1960s brought a lot of squatters and druggies to the house. Since it was abandoned at that point, nobody cared what went on there. By 1965, Gravenfrost Asylum underwent a regime change, and the head, a guy named Edgar Colbrook, registered the house as a historical site. He and the Mayor pulled some strings, and got the GFPD and several other county law enforcement agencies to clear the place out. Sounded like overkill, right? Maybe to someone who wasn't up on their history. They only found twelve people squatting there. Just twelve, and they were more than happy to get the hell out.

The rest of the tenants were liquefying in the basement. Forty, all told.

They had to hire a company from New Jersey, who had never heard of the joint, to come clean the house and restore it. Doctor Colbrook wanted to use the house as a place his resident doctors and their families could stay. Nobody played ball. So again, it sat for nearly a decade—used as campfire story fodder and double-dog-dares on Halloween. Who can get the closest? Can you touch the doorknob? Can you stand on the porch and say "Devil's Domicile" ten times without shot-putting a terror turd in your drawers?

After being pressed by the board of trustees, Dr. Colbrook reluctantly put the house up for sale, in hopes of recouping some of the money they lost in its restoration. Surprise, surprise, nobody was interested. Couple more years went by, and our boy Lincoln Travers came along. The Asylum pretty much gave him the house to take care of. Hell, they may have even paid him—they've had enough. As I shuffled through the horrific Travers Travesty photos, I couldn't help but feel like Travers was drawn to the house somehow. Like it called to him all those miles away. He was honing his skills on the road, and now he had a place that was begging to be fed. Travers, that sick son of a dick, was the goddamn delivery boy. After the Travesty, the house fell back into the reluctant hands of the Asylum, and resumed being a horror hot spot. From what I understand, the GF is no stranger to missing persons and assorted creature features—but as far as the local government was concerned, the Domicile wasn't involved.

I had enough horror and gore for one night. I jammed the photos back into the folder, put the cork back into the bottle, and turned the lamp off. The light from the parking lot oozed through the curtains and coated the room like lung infection phlegm. I stared at a painting of a child on a tire swing that hung above the TV across the room. As I drifted off, I noticed several sets of feet dangling above her head—swaying. The little girl's face began to melt. I chuckled and flipped her off.

Nighty-night, little Susies.

4
THE THREE PENDÈJOS

Morning came like a punch to the dick. I dragged myself to the shower, and it was then I noticed the two-tone tub. The bottom-to-rib level was copper. Squeaky clean, mind you, just forever stained by countless lost causes looking for a one way ticket off this spinning space rock. All those sad, sad ghosts...

...looking up at my balls.

As Buk and I headed to the car, I glanced over at the cemetery. In the distance, a man, tall and wide like an oak tree, stood by a mausoleum and just... well, stood there. He was too far off to get a good look at, not that it mattered. As soon as I let Buk into the car and turned back to look, he was gone. Couldn't tell you for certain if was really there in the first place or not.

"On a gathering storm comes a tall handsome man—in a dusty black coat with a red, right hand." I said. Buk barked once. "Nick Cave and The Bad Seeds, pal. We heard it on the way up. Don't act like you don't know." I fired the engine up and we headed toward the diner. Hunger and hangover wouldn't be denied.

*

We staggered into Grant's Diner like two Bedouin from a sandstorm. A voluptuous waitress straight out of a '50s pinup calendar smiled and said that my party was waiting for me.

"My what?"

"You're friend had been waiting for you about an hour and a half. Said he was meeting a handsome fella and his handsome pup. That must be you, right?" She leaned over to give Buk a scratch behind the ears. His tail was wagging like crazy, and by the sight of her ample bosom, mine was threatening to do the same. I looked toward the booths and Parker Powell waved. Buk ran over to him like a goddamned turncoat, and hopped up next to him.

"What's your name, beautiful?" I asked the bombshell, whose likeness could have been on the side of a World War II plane that was bombing the shit out of the enemy.

"I'm Annie." She smiled. We shook hands.

"Special Agent Bobby Doyle, at your service."

"Well, Special Bobby, coffee is on the house. Have a seat and I'll be right with you." She was a Rockabilly beauty, all right—complexion like fresh snow, and her hair was chocolate brown all pulled back into a red bandanna. I wanted to tell her about my Charger, about roller derby, about the things I'm not afraid to do to please a woman. You know, small talk. But etiquette dictated that I wait until after the check. So instead, I smiled and walked over to the two star-crossed lovers, Parker and Bukowski.

"Morning, Agent Doyle," Parker stuck out his

hand. This time I shook it. What the hell, right? You can only be so much of a dick so much of the time.

"Mr. Powell..." I sat across from him and spun the menu on the table.

"Call me Parker."

"Alright. Parker. How'd you know I'd be coming here?"

"When a person is new to a town, and doesn't know the little breakfast spots, they come to the diner. Diners are a safe bet."

"Investigative reporting at its finest. Looks like you're a hell of a dog thief too."

"This guy?" Parker chuckled and rubbed Buk on the noggin. "He's my buddy, right? Right?" Buk barked in agreement. "I can't help it if he's got good taste."

"Here you go, Special." Annie set the coffee down and refilled Parker's cup. "Get you boys some breakfast?"

"You have one of those dishes with the quirky name and a shit-ton of food?"

"That'd be the Gravedigger. Two Eggs, four pieces of bacon with four pieces of sausage, or two slices of ham, four flapjacks or two pieces of challah bread French toast with home fries."

"Yes. That. Scrambled—bacon and sausage—French toast. Judas mutt, here, will have ham and hash if you got it."

"You bet, honey. And for you, Parker?" She knew him?

"Pepper omelet, wheat toast, no potatoes." Annie nodded and took her leave.

"Not much of a breakfast." I sipped the beautiful, black coffee.

"Eating big isn't conducive to living in a Winnebago." He took a sip of his own coffee, light and sweet. Tsk. "The toilet can only hold so much, and the vent system only takes the tang off it. And the Walmart bathroom has a layer of piss-dappled and shit-flecked schmegma on the floor and seats by the time I get to them."

"I'm *so* happy to know that."

"Hey, *you* brought it up." He winked. "So what did you think?"

"'Bout what?"

"About the stuff I gave you. And the footage. Freaky shit, right?"

"How do you know about the footage? You saw it?"

"Who do you think edited it?"

"Bull. What, they just handed federal investigation evidence over to a civilian?"

"Actually, we did." Deputy Walker tapped me on the shoulder. I scooted in a bit, and he sat. He left his coat in the car, and I was able to get a look at his build. The boy worked out, that's for sure. Like an actor whose job is to look continually perfect for a role—muscular yet slender—size but no bulk. Guess I didn't notice in the precinct's fluorescent lighting, but in the diner lighting?

I hated him.

Annie bee-lined over to him and kissed him on the mouth. I hated him even more.

"This guy giving you a problem, Special? Damn pigs in this town need a good frisking." She laughed and topped off our cups.

"The only pigs I want to see are on a plate, ma'am, or you'll get a touch of police brutality." Walker pulled her in for another kiss.

"Yes sir, Deputy Husband, sir." Annie saluted. "Your orders'll be up soon, boys."

"Thanks, Annie." Parker smiled. She tended to

another table, I tried not to look too disappointed.

"Deputy husband, huh?" I slurped my coffee obnoxiously.

"Coming up on three years this December." Walker smiled.

"Mazel tov. So, before I have the two of you dragged before a federal judge for tampering with murder evidence, why don't we cut the Blue's Clues bullshit and get to the real cock-and-balls of the situation? Let's start with you, Walker. And remember, I'm an all-powerful super federal-type guy."

"I'm sorry for misleading you, Doyle. If I didn't cloak-and-dagger this, then nothing would have been done. Sheriff Laidlaw is a good man, but he's too status quo. Bunch of kids go to The Domicile and get themselves whacked? Whether it was a drug related rampage, or a suicide pact, he'd want to brush it under the rug best he could. Pin Zane Bagley as the bad guy, lock him up, and call it a day. You'll see, Bagley isn't going to argue in his own defense. There's footage of him actively killing three people. Use that and only that, and you got a home run."

"He'd do that?"

"Not for himself. But the Mayor—"

"Mayor Frank McGann, right?"

"Right. He's like the Mayor from *Jaws*," Parker nodded. "The beach stays open—to hell with the man-eating shark."

"Forgive me, but what kind of tourist draw does this burgh have that could possibly be threatened by another Domicile death? I've barely heard of this place until I was sent here."

"Honestly? Not much. But McGann has been trying to change that. You saw the Starbucks?"

"I did."

"There's a Walmart across the bridge, too. The powers that be want to gentrify Gravenfrost, and make it a seaside destination. They want to build a resort, and more restaurants and shops. They have high hopes, and murder tends to be a dog turd in the boot tread of progress." Walker sipped his coffee. Annie set our meals down and we all clammed up like we were covering up some kind of dark conspiracy.

"Oh, that's how it is? The Three Schmucketeers and Barktanion? Good luck getting a refill now." She smiled. Walker caressed her arm with the back of his hand, and I understood—this was more than just a job. Gravenfrost was his home. He was a guy trying to build a life on ground that was more bone than dirt.

"Look, the last thing I want to do is get Laidlaw in trouble. He was a great sheriff in his time, and he's seen his fair share of crazy Gravenfrost shit. He just wants to keep his head down and retire."

"He was one of the responding officers at the Travers Travesty." Parker chewed his omelet.

"No shit?" I chewed my sausage.

"Woof!" Buk chewed his ham.

"He must have been a young'un."

"Fresh out of the academy," Walker nodded. "To this day, he still won't talk about it."

"No doubt. Where do you come into all this, Powell?" I emptied my cup. Walker waved to Annie, who just shook her head.

"Nope. You get it yourself." she said. Walker got up, went behind the counter and took the pot. He returned and filled our cups then moved along the tables, topping off the other patrons. A Boy Scout.

"I moved to the Frost after a near-death experience in South Carolina. Some local mook recognized me from the L'Brano hit order, and tried to off me. That's when I bought the 'Bago and headed North. I couldn't stay in one place for too long—I needed to be mobile. So far, it's worked out. I introduced myself to Bruce and Laidlaw as a courtesy. I figured it was only right to give them a heads up in case something went down—and maybe they'd lend a hand if it did. Bruce and I became friends, so I stayed and give the GFPD some detective help when they need it. I still write articles from time-to-time, fluff stuff mostly. I'm still living off the fat checks I got from my exposé and the TV interviews and whatnot. And you'd be surprised how much money you save by not throwing it at someone to occupy space that you do not own."

"You mean rent?"

"Rent, yeah."

"Why didn't you just say rent?"

"I get paid by the word, pal. So, like I was saying... Bruce and I became friends and we work cases together. I guess I'm like a consultant."

"Guess that'd make me the *insultant*." Neither of them laughed. Dicks. "Alright, so you two do a little Hardy Boys action, and suddenly you get dibs on murder evidence? Little convenient, no?"

"Let me put it out on the table, Doyle; I'm the reason you're here. This is bigger than anything Bruce and I have ever handled, and we needed the FBI's spooky fun-time agent. If I didn't make a few calls, you'd still be chasing Goy Gothog cultists around Rhode Island."

"You know about that?" I was actually impressed.

"Yep. And I also know about Chinatown."

"...Oh."

"Just saying that I have a lot of info on a lot of people, and a phone book's worth of contacts. We needed you here. Your record speaks for itself. You're a do-whatever-it-takes kind of guy, and so are we. We need to end this Dickinson shit once and for all."

"You had me at *rent*, super sleuth. Why'd you take so long to tell me you were in love with me?"

"Phhhht!" Parker flipped me off. Walker took a

bite out of his farmer's omelet.

"So, Brucy Bruce, you feel like spelunking in The Domicile after we see Zane Bagley?" Walker went rigid.

"I don't... I can't go in there." He gripped the table tight.

"How are you going to be any help if you-—"

"I got a call few years back..." Walker's eyes went all fuzzy, like he was there instead of here. "I was sent there on a gunfire complaint. Nobody lives near the house, but some woman was jogging and she heard a scream, then a single shot. An all-points was put out and I was the closest. I got there in less than three minutes, and after a quick what's what from the complainant, I ran past the cursing stones and went in."

"Cursing stones?"

"People would write a name of the person they hated on a rock or a brick, and toss it near the house. They think the evil will seep into it and curse whoever's on it. You'll see, the lawn is nearly paved with them." Parker stated.

"I should have waited for backup," Walker continued, "but I was still pretty new. I still had a bit of what they call John Wayne or Dirty Harry syndrome. I felt sick as soon as I entered, like I was in a dryer tumbling over myself. I heard whimpering coming from the second floor, so I slowly went up. I peered around the hallway opening and it was just so dark, like, unnaturally so. Nothing could be that dark. It wasn't just the absence of light, but the absence of hope. There was a door midway down the hall that slowly creaked open and spilled out bile-yellow light. Gun drawn, I made my way down as quietly as I could. The whimpering amplified, along with angry whispers. Each step brought more dread, like I was waiting for a balloon to pop. I reached the door, and spun in.

"Freeze!" I shouted, but I was the one who

froze. On the bed was my younger brother Matt, and laying by his side was his girlfriend Tabitha, who was missing a portion of her face. Matt held our father's snub-nosed 38 in both hands and looked so vacant.

"M-Matty?" I whispered. He looked up, with eyes that switched between deep sorrow and panic. I holstered my gun and approached him with my hands out as if I were sneaking up to catch a bird. "Put Daddy's gun down. What are you doing here, Matty? Just...put it down, okay?" He pointed it at me and my hands began to shake. "It's gonna be okay."

"You don't get it!" He shouted. "Nothing is nothing! They said so! They said this house will keep us together, and that we don't have to be apart!"

"Who? Who told you that bullshit?" I shouted. I was angry and scared and out of my depth. Matty looked over my shoulder.

"They did." I spun, thinking someone was there. I could feel it, you know? There was nobody. I turned back to my sixteen-year-old brother and gasped. He held Tabitha's limp hand and shoved the barrel into his mouth... and..." Walker wiped his mouth with the napkin and took a gulp of water.

"I don't know what came over me. I tried CPR. What could I do? My little brother needed me, and I went into autopilot. With each chest compression, his brain lurched further out of the hole he made, and I could hear the laughter. Something, someone was fucking laughing at me. I hadn't even realized that the other deputies pulled me from Matt until I was outside. I fought like hell to get back to him. I don't remember what happened after that. Shock is a funny thing, huh? Week later, we had the wake and funeral. Tabitha's family blamed my family—my family blamed them back—both settled on blaming me, which I was already doing myself. Laidlaw gave me an open-ended convalescence to cope. Some said I should buy a motorcycle and see the country. Others said I should hike the Appalachian Trail. My father didn't give a shit what I did, as long as it was far away from him. Tabitha's mom suggested that I eat a bullet. Still does. So you can imagine, Doyle, how badly I want the deaths to stop. That place needs to be cleansed or buried. Something to end it once and for all. I'll do whatever I need to help you accomplish that, but please, don't ask me to set one foot back in that fucking house."

"Shit, Bruce, I—"

"You're a smoker, right?" I nodded. "Give me one." I pulled the pack from my jacket and tapped it on the table, causing a single cig to pop up. An old shaman trick. Walker plucked it and put it to his lips as he stood. "Finish up, we have to get to the Asylum." He walked past the register and took a complimentary matchbook. Annie rushed to our table looking ready to bust heads.

"Is Bruce *smoking*? What did you assholes say to him?" She didn't wait for a response. She stormed out of the diner and confronted her man. I felt like a douche as I watched her console him. The level of love those two shared was remarkable. They hugged as the whole diner looked on. Walker flicked the cigarette to the ground and kissed Annie hard—real hard, like in a movie, then pulled his cruiser out of the parking lot. After he was gone, Annie glared at me through the window. I was a kid sitting in the principal's office. Parker and I rose to leave as Annie came back in. She waved off the concerns of the cashier and smiled politely as she approached us.

"You assholes are going to make this right," she whispered. Parker and I nodded. "You're going to do whatever it takes to solve this thing, and put souls to rest, right?"

"Well, it's not exactly that—" I began. Annie grabbed me and pulled me in squishy-close. I could smell her body lotion. It was noticeable but faint, and I bet it had a poetic name like "Moonlight Tongue Punch." Men's scents are ridiculously named. Like the companies want to over-butch the names to compensate for smelling like a disinfectant. *New "Thinking Lava Stallion!" Or, try "Wolfballs Overnight Musk!" Smell like a woodland creature tea-bagged your forehead!*

Anyway.

"Make it right, Special," she said. "You couldn't possibly know the pain he's felt."

"I wish you were right." I looked her straight in the eye, and she saw I meant it. She let me go and fixed my lapel.

"Just..." she searched for the words. I placed my hand on her shoulder and smiled softly. She nodded, and I paid the bill at the register. I kept the receipt for reimbursement, by the way.

"Mind if I ride with you?" Parker asked. Bukowski sat by his feet, and I wanted to catapult them both into the sea. "My whip isn't exactly a—"

"Pussy magnet? Yeah, I can kind of see that. Sure, let's go." I hopped in as Parker helped Buk into the back seat. As I pulled from the spot, I saw Annie serving a customer with her best game face on. Walker had found himself one hell of a woman. The odds of finding someone like her ran through my head, and I frowned. Hell, I can't even stop my dog from falling for another man. How in the hell could I find a Mrs. Bobby Doyle?

"Chinatown, right?"

"What?"

"When you and Annie were talking about pain, you were thinking of Chinatown. That's rough, man. I read the file on that and how you—" I lit a cig and puffed like mad, filling the cabin with smoke. Parker valiantly fought the cough that brewed in his burning lungs. He tried to roll the window down but I had locked them. He gave in and coughed so hard he damn-near vomited.

"Okay! OKAY! I get it!" he choked. "Touchy subject!" I'm—*wheeze*—sorry!" I unlocked the window, and he rolled it down and gulped fresh air like a guppy. The rest of the ride was mercifully quiet.

5
THE JUST US LEAGUE

Gravenfrost Asylum sat like a tombstone. With the Atlantic behind it, it looked like the final boss in a video game. Ominous and brutal. Grayer than an old woman's nipple and half as inviting, it cut a chunk out of the darkening sky where a storm threatened to pummel us all to hell. The medical hospital sat against the asylum like a parasitic twin, squat and malnourished. Its host fed on chaos, not healing.

An ambulance rushed past us as we parked in the visitor's lot, and screeched around the circular drive where, in the middle, statues of Dr. Cattell and Dr. Olson stood like proud poppas. I left the window open for Buk, regardless of the impending storm. I figured rainwater on the upholstery was better than dog squeezin's.

"Storm's a-brewin'," I said in my best, salty sea dog voice.
"Yar, looks purdy bard," Parker replied. He's alright for a dog thief. I could feel the weight of dread increase with every step. Barred windows, gargoyles

overlooking the island like grim observers of man's folly. I figured it must be how Batman felt each time he went to Arkham Asylum. *How long until they lock me up with the rest of the nuts?* He *was* dressed like a bat, and all.

The lobby was a large concrete rotunda with two doors to either side of the enclosed reception desk, where a despondent worker sat. Walker stood at the door to the left, marked Administration. The skinny woman with thick-rimmed glasses didn't bother to look up through the shatterproof window as we approached.

"That them?" she said. Imagine a perfectly normal person who had been tranquilized, and is speaking while pinching their nose. That's our receptionist.

"Yes, that's them."

"Step through the door when you hear the buzz. There's a guard booth where you can check your sidearms, knives, pens, keys and anything else that may be a potential threat..."

BZZZZZZZZZZZZT—Ka-CHUNK! The door unlocked. Walker and Parker stepped through, but I just had to see what was so damn interesting that she wouldn't bother to look up. She was reading a book. Not just *any* book, mind you...

"*Trailblazers of Lust?*"

"So?" she shrugged, eyes ever upon the page.

"I've read that one."

"You have?" That got her attention.

"Yeah, it's sad. Snake gets ass-cancer of the mouth, and Stone has to man the ranch by himself while Tanya decides to run off with Don Gazpacho."

"Thanks, DICKHEAD!" she shouted and tossed

the book at the window. I smiled like the Cheshire Cat and walked through the door.

"You actually read that shit, man?" Parker asked.

"Pfft, yeah, right." I slapped his shoulder. "Just a lucky guess. Every character in the history of that genre is named Stone, or Snake, or Stone Snake. And come on, *ass cancer of the mouth*?"

"Ha! Yeah, wow! I can't believe she fell for it."

Note to self: Burn autographed copy of *Trailblazers of Lust*.

There was a metal detector manned by a guy who made Big Bad Leroy Brown look like moderately-sizable and pleasant to be around Mr. Brown. His name was Marvin, and did I mention he was big?

"Mornin' fellas," he said. "Deputy."

"Marvin, how are you?"

"Notha' day above ground, namean? You know the drill." He held out a plastic tray where Walker placed his service pistol and back up revolver in. After he dropped his cuffs into it, I did the same. Parker placed a tiny can of pepper spray and his car keys.

"Don't forget your rape whistle," I said. Marvin laughed. I thought it was the sound of a wall collapsing. Parker blushed.

"I'll lock these up. Ya'll know where you're headed?"

"Yes, we have a meeting at nine with Dr. Lydia Hobbs." Walker nodded. Marvin frowned.

"You're late. She's gonna have your ass. Best of luck, fellas," he chuckled. We walked down the off-white corridor, past the employee cafeteria, mail room, and HR department, and pressed the button for one of two elevators. I felt the need to apologize to Walker for earlier. I guess I was getting soft.

"Sorry about... you know. Before."

"Don't worry about it. You didn't know, and I could have handled it better."

"No, hey, it was a terrible goddamned thing. And I promise you, we'll get to the bottom of this shit."

"We never did get to talk about what you thought of the footage," Parker said, ever on the job.

"Not now. Not here. Later. Beer." I stated.

"Beer," Walker agreed. Parker shrugged as the elevator doors opened. A skinny waif of a man stood inside with a metal clipboard and a paisley tie. His youthful eyes attempted to glower at us with hilarious results.

"You're late!" Yelled the waif.

"Who the hell does this pipsqueak think he's talking to?" I said. He recoiled slightly, then recomposed his ire. We stepped into the elevator, nearly shoving him against the wall. Walker reached for the fifth floor button, but Waifly the Waif, smacked his hand.

"We're going to the basement level. Dr. Hobbs waited in her office for ten extra minutes—*waiting for you*—and I'm afraid she's very cross. She is currently with Mr. Bagley in one of the holding rooms." He pressed the button and the door closed. "I can't *believe* how late you are."

"Easy, kid." I said. Waifly spun on his heel.

"I'm no kid! I'm twenty-eight! He bristled.

"I'd be impressed if his voice didn't just crack." Parker laughed.

"It most certainly did not, Mr. Powell."

"You've heard of me?"

"I've read your work."

"Oh? What did you think?"

"Eh." shrugged Waifly.

"You look eighteen." Parker grunted.

"And a half," I added with a thumbs up.

"I should expect nothing less from civil servants." Waifly jutted his nose in the air.

The dick had spunk, I'll—no, scratch that last sentence from the tape. That's tasteless even for me. Why are you laughing, Agent Remender?

"You know anything about law enforcement?" Walker asked.

"I have an *advanced* degree, so, no."

"See, when you get an unruly perp, sometimes you have to take your time. Make sure you secured him properly." Walker leaned in close to Waifly's ear. "Sometimes you have to get creative, see? Get hands on. Really make the son of a bitch wish his daddy wore a rubber. These things can take time, you understand?" Waifly was stiff as a board, as he nodded in quick bursts.

"You think that biker'll ever eat solid food again?" I played into the ruse. Parker raspberried the air and laughed.

"Not unless those were his baby teeth, and he's expecting another batch."

"What can I say?" Walker laughed. "He got lippy. I hate lippy." The door opened and Waifly stumbled out, pressing the clipboard to his crotch.

"I think our boy is sporting wood." I said.

"Aw, what the hell?" Walker grimaced. We could hear Zane's screams as soon as we stepped from the elevator. A strong female voice was also heard, stabbing words into his howls with condescension.

"Parker, record this," I whispered.

"Been recording since the lobby." He winked.

"Ah... right this w-way, gentlemen." Waifly pointed and shuffled off, trying to keep his mule in check with the clipboard. He dropped it, making an echoing clatter against the tile floor. Each time he reached for it, he kicked it further down the hall. The female voice stopped. The holding cell door opened, and out walked a woman about five-ten, pale white skin and midnight black hair done up in a bun with two strands framing her model-beautiful face. And her body? It'd make Sir Mix-A-Lot stutter. She wore a form-fitting charcoal gray suit with a puffy white blouse that accentuated her... stuff. She pulled her sexy librarian glasses down and looked at Waifly with angry, dark brown eyes.

"Jeremy! Are you tumescent?!" Her voice was out of a foreign film where every character was a poet and sex fiend. Barbed wire made from velvet. Waifly (no, I don't care his name is Jeremy) picked his clipboard up and pressed it to his schmeckle. I immediately understood their relationship. Waifly was a submissive, and boss lady was the whip-cracking dominatrix. He got off on being treated like shit. The way she glowered at him, like a cat looking at a cricket, was intense.

"Hey, Jer, lemme borrow the clipboard, willya?" I whispered.

"I assume this is the federal agent you insisted I meet, Deputy Walker?" She pierced me with those eyes.

"Yes, ma'am. Special Agent Robert Doyle, this is Doctor Lyd—"

"Doctor Lydia Hobbs, Head Doctor and Chief of Staff for this facility." She shook my hand as a professional courtesy, but there was nothing behind it. You can tell a lot from someone's handshake, and from hers I could tell that she'd rather be lancing boils on a fat man's ass with her teeth than help us with the investigation.

"Head Doctor. Kind of ironic, right?" I smiled.

"Beg your pardon?"

"You're the *head* doctor in a loony bin. Head."

"Yes, very droll," Hobbs shook her head.

"And not ironic," added Waifly. "Pedantic at best."

65

"Would that count as lippy, Deputy?" I asked.

"Oooh, yes..." Walker cracked his knuckles. Waifly *eeped* and moved behind the doctor.

"Mr. Bagley is extremely volatile at the moment," Hobbs said. "He is not responding well to the sedatives we have provided. I fear he's had a total psychological schism. I strongly advise against—"

"Thank you, Doctor, but I'm afraid I'll have to speak with him regardless."

"Sole survivor of a multiple homicide who has clearly lost his mind? You needn't look too long for the killer. He's right in that room." If she only knew what I knew. In a way, she was correct. Zane was responsible for several deaths, but not all, and certainly not without just cause. But again, she couldn't have known. To her, this whole thing fits perfectly into a box. Maybe she was just pissed to have another high profile patient in her hospital.

"That reminds me," I smiled. "Lincoln Travers is still here, right?"

"He is. But why—?"

"I'm going to need to speak with him as well."

"Outrageous!" she balled her fists. She was so hot. And a total bitch. My kind of woman. I got in real close and smiled. I could smell her—lavender, honey, and candle wax.

"With all due respect, Doctor, I'm going to speak with Travers whether you agree to it or not. As a professional courtesy, I asked nicely. Interfering with a federal investigation will not only get you removed from your current position here at the hospital, but may actually relocate you to a federal prison. And let me say, you'll find prison to be very... what was the word you used, Jer?"

"Pedantic."

"Pedantic! So, again, with respect, do as I ask." I winked and she exhaled so sharply that I could tell she had been clenching every muscle in her body. She wanted to rip me a new one, but I had her dead-to-rights. She was a control freak in a building full of chaos, who had just lost the final say in the matter. I understood her frame of mind—if she didn't exert total control every single second, she felt the place would crumble around her. I could appreciate that. But I had a job to do.

Underline that in your notes. That's a good line for the bosses.

"Yes, fine." Hobbs conceded. "Jeremy, arrange Travers to be brought to room five here."

"Yes, Doctor." Waifly scooted back to the elevators and glared menacingly at me. I kissed the air.

"Thank you, Doctor." I nodded. "Now, if you don't mind?" I motioned toward room six, where Zane was. She swiped her ID badge, and the magnetic lock sharply clicked. I opened the door and Walker stepped between Hobbs and the room.

"What are you doing?"

"FBI stuff, Doc. No interference." Walker closed the door behind me and Parker.

"Preposterous," she said through the door.

*

Zane Bagley sat restrained to a padded chair bolted to the floor. Parker and I sat in our own bolted chairs on the other side of the bolted table. The fluorescent lighting bathed the grayish-white room a sickly irradiated ambiance. Zane was dressed in a gray version of the DOC's tacky orange jumpsuits, and twitched like he was being tickled by a cattle prod. His eyes darted around the room as if he was tracking a fly. Parker removed the recorder from his coat pocket and set it on the table, then gave me a *now what*? look.

"Mr. Bagley..." I began. His attention was everywhere else but on me. "Mr. Bagley?" Nothing. "ZANE!" I smacked the metal table, causing him and piss pants Parker to jump. Now I had his attention.

"Mr. Bagley, Zane, I'm Special Agent Robert Doyle of the FBI. This is Parker Powell, my... what are you, Powell?"

"I'm his consultant," he said to Zane.

"He's my piss boy."

"Doyle, this is recording," Parker motioned to the recorder. I picked it up and stated for the record:

"Parker Powell is my piss boy."

"Very nice. Real professional."

"Listen, Zane, we want you to know that—"

"Gonna GET me! Gonna GET ME!" Zane howled.

"Nobody's gonna get you, pal." I assured him. He shook his head quickly and tried to sink into the chair.

"...Gonna."

"We know you killed those people out of self-defense. I know they were once your friends and something terrible happened to them. You have to trust us, okay? We're on your side."

"They c-came from thuh-the walls." Zane managed to say without shouting in terror. "The shadow people. From the walls. Ghosts fruh-from the floors and ceilings and walls and shelves and mirrors and faces OH GOD, THE FACES! Lady in shadows! The Lady in shadows!"

"Easy, Zane. What about the lady in the shadows?"

"S-s-said I fuh-failed. S-said gonna get me."

"Well, *fuck* her, right?" I slapped the table again. "You got out of the horrible place! You didn't fail a damn thing! I don't give a shit who said so, okay? I'm

68

going to get to the bottom of all this, and then get you out of here." Zane's eyes lit up. "We're gonna get you some quality help. I know Dr. Hobbs's booty is mighty fine, but I'd feel better if you let *my* people take care of you. That alright?"

"Yes, p-p-please," he whispered. He looked over his shoulders like he was about to begin telling a racist joke. "Not safe here. Gonna get me."

"You'll be fine. Anything happens to you and I tear the place down. Now I need you to focus. I need you to tell me what you saw. What you heard, anything that can help me figure out what I'm dealing with. Did you hear any strange languages? Names that stood out? Tell me more about the shadow people."

"Lady in shadows—man in shadows. Midnight black full of hunger the house feeds—eats minds and blood and skin and bones and eyes and happiness and sadness and souls and life and death and death and death and death." His eyes went back to tracking imaginary flies. I stood and slowly walked behind him. My palms hovered above his head, and I took several deep breaths.

"Listen to me now... you are protected by the white light. Close your eyes, breathe slowly and breathe deep. Feel the protective light wash over you like a waterfall, cleansing you of darkness, of shadows, of negativity. The light is your armor, and the darkness cannot penetrate it no matter what. Only positive energy may enter. Feel it building inside you like a fire, and emanating like the rays of the sun. These rays protect you and keep the darkness at bay. Only you can turn it off. Don't turn it off, Zane. Keep it bright." Tears ran down his cheeks, and his posture relaxed. The mind is the most powerful element. Positive will heal—negative will sicken. Snarky Asshole—the mindset I'm most accustomed to—keeps me menza menz.

"Thank you," Zane whispered. I could hear the clarity in his voice.

"No problem." I walked back to my chair but didn't sit. There was nothing more Zane could tell me. Nothing the tapes didn't already reveal.

"The white light will help you, but you got to keep protecting yourself with it. Even, hell, *especially* in this place." It wasn't going to heal his troubled mind, but it eased it some. No small thing.

"Okay..."

"Repeat after me: I am protected by the white light."

"I am p-protected by the wh-white light."

"Good. Now stay strong. I'll be back for you when all this is over." I tapped Parker on the shoulder and he got up. I tapped on the door and Dr. Hobbs opened it with a scowl.

"Travers ready?"

"Yes, but I *must* protest."

"Duly noted—duly ignored. You ready, Mr. Consultant?"

"Oh, now I'm your consultant." Parker laughed. "That was pretty amazing, by the way."

"What?"

"The white light thing. He was like a normal person again."

"It's spiritual healing and protection. Anyone can do it, really. And whether it's—"

"Hogwash," Dr. Hobbs interjected.

"Or power of the mind, the results are palpable."

"New Age nonsense. There's no evidence supporting spiritual healing."

"Ask a Buddhist. Or better yet, Zane Bagley." I said. I wasn't looking forward to speaking to the notorious Lincoln Travers, but I had to know if anything he said would jive with the current events. Parker and I stood in front of room number five like two priests preparing do go an exorcism. Hobbs opened the door and we went in.

"Why is it so dark?" asked Parker.

"Mr. Travers is a bit photo-sensitive. Hence the one functioning fluorescent track bulb." She slammed the door, cutting Parker and I off from the rest of the world. We were now in the realm of Dick-n-Die himself, who sat in the half-light looking like the illegitimate love child of Jim Morrison and Charles Manson. He had a wild mane of salt and pepper hair that wove nicely into his bushy beard. His eyes were pin pricks in the shadow of his face. He hung his head to obscure his features and add to the menace. Parker sat down first, which initially surprised me. But he was the dude who faced down gangsters with his words and brass balls. Travers, by Parker's viewpoint, was nothing more than a cartoon villain. Decades in the booby-hatch did little to quell his presence, though. Now that he was pushing sixty, he had time to hone his gifts. The air popped with tension. I could feel the gravity around us swirling, pulling, trying to get its sticky fingers around our throats. He was getting to me and he didn't say a goddamned word. Parker set the recorder down and nodded.

"Mr. Travers, I'm Special Agent D—"

"*RHEE RHEE RHEE!*" Travers squealed like a, well, you get it.

"That's a lovely singing voice. You should have started a band instead of a cult." I adjusted my tie for no good reason. I didn't want to admit that Travers was getting to me. Just something about that toolbag set me on edge—ready to fall.

"The angels on their bloodied knees—supplicant idolatry. How they adore us. How they mourn us. Oh, my, how they *failed* us." His voice sounded like a late night love song DJ. I could see how he was a successful cult leader and all around shit zipper.

"Yeah, how 'bout that? Anyway, I was wondering if you could answer a few questions for—"

"—Entreaties seeking admonition."

"Right, so... how about it?" I shrugged. He stared at me lovingly as a father would, and splayed his fingers on the table. "The Devil's Domicile."

"Home."

"Tell me if you can, what's truly happening there? I understand who you are and what you've done, but—"

"Do you? Truly? Perhaps teacher can explain the farrago before him to the farrago before him."

"Sure, as soon as I get my thesaurus." I gave him a thumbs up. "The Dickinson house—what significance did it have on your... work?" His face lit up with a smile. Megalomaniacs like Travers loved to have their sickness labeled as work, or passion. Makes it seem as though they aren't just scum.

"Home called to me from across the great expanse. Beckoned me to take my religion to the holiest of altars. The parish of perish—where spirits of chaos and horror, the hosts of immaculate and ejaculate pain and suffering are immured. The carnal chapel in red, red gory glory called unto me like a dinner bell, and we were both so very hungry. We feed on death, you see. Born screaming into this world by suffering madness."

"Dickinson built the place to house madness." Parker said. Travers smiled.

"No, love, to *grow* it! Every window, stud and nail is madness! Each carpet fiber, wine glass and dust mote is imbued with stark raving lunacy!"

"Who's Cyrus?" I jumped in, hoping to catch him off guard, and to truly test his knowledge of what only few people know. Travers leaned back and clicked his tongue.

"A nihil ad rem tawny fleck of a spirit. But he was one of the originals, and therefore deserves respect."

"He was one of the patients who built the house?" I played ignorant.

"Oh, yes! I do believe he's part of the mortar

72

these days. Heh! The others are worse by far, and plentiful." Travers drummed his fingers on the table.

"Tell me about the Lady in Shadow."

"Whom?"

"Lady in Shadow. Or the Man in Shadow. What can you tell me about them?"

"Nothing."

"Bullshit."

"Nothing, Agent Piggie-Pig. They must be new additions that the old tenants didn't mention. Which is irritating, really."

"Why's that?"

"I was destined to be one with that house. I was meant to be assimilated and take my place among the Marquis of macabre. You see, my gift? My gift is that I can see the very souls of every living thing. Like a soft glow beneath the skin just *begging* to be freed. That is my calling. Once I fed the house with enough souls, I would take my place among those princes of perdition. But I failed. Much like they say the little soul in the other room has. Yet another failure... and my, are they displeased!"

"Interesting," Parker said. "So you are still able to speak with the spirits in the house."

"Not *in* the house! They *are* the house! The house is alive, you see."

"Well, you tell them..." I tough-guyed it as I stood. "You tell them I'm coming for them."

"Oh, they already know. They are very much looking forward to it. By the by, Agent Piggie-Pig, they say a great change is imminent for you. The noble cognomen designated shall be Bobby Bones."

"That means I'm either going to die or become a porn star," I shrugged. "I don't take much stock in the ethereal rantings of deceased half-wits."

"Your hubris is why you'll fail."

"Okay, pal, thanks for your time and eloquent

bullshit." I knocked on the door. It buzzed and I opened it.

"It is a house of *pain*, pig!" Travers offered his parting wisdom.

"Then I'll be sure to jump up, jump up and get down." Travers looked terribly confused.

"I don't think he got the reference," Parker said as we walked from the room. "He's been in here since, like, the '70s."

"You got it though, right?"

"Yeah."

"It was contextually funny, right?"

"Meh." Parker shrugged.

"Fucking critics," I sighed. Walker smiled at me like he was in on a joke I didn't get. Dr. Hobbs slipped a piece of paper in my breast pocket.

"This is my address. I expect you six o'clock sharp. I will prepare an elegant meal to make up for my attitude. It's been quite stressful the past few days, and I feel I should apologize." She smiled. I didn't think it was possible, but she did. A match struck in the darkness, brilliant, yet elegant and small. God, she was beautiful.

"I do like food," I muttered like a dope. Parker looked at me with a *you lucky sumbitch* smirk, while Waifly tried to light my head on fire with the power of his mind. If anything, I had to accept the invitation just to screw with that sniveling tampon. "Alright, six it is."

"Sharp." Hobbs nodded.

"—*ish*." I winked. The match blew out. Her smile was gone.

*

Parker's Winnebago was one of those deluxe jammies that old folks tool around in once they retire and have no interest babysitting their douchebag kids' douchebag kids. It had three pull-out beds—one of which he converted into a mini Batcave—and a modest kitchen/eating area equipped with a diner-esque booth, where the three of us sat, killing a bottle of Graves End whiskey. We discussed the pressing matters at hand.

"You're going to need condoms," Parker said.

"It's just dinner. I can't imagine anything else happening," I shrugged. "She's not exactly the most inviting person."

"You didn't see what I saw," Walker swished the ice cubes in his tumbler full of iced tea, and stared at them as they spun. He wasn't a drinker like me and Parker. Which is probably a good thing. "She's not used to people talking back to her. I couldn't tell if she wanted to deck you or make you strap her on like a feedbag."

"Poetic," I raised my glass. "Alright, I'll bring a couple jimmy-caps in case her—what was it called?— Georgia O'Keefe isn't surrounded by barbed wire and claymores."

"The hell did you just call her puss?" Parker snorted.

"It was what Walker's secretary called hers."

"Angie..." Walker shook his head. "She's a nut." Someone knocked on the door. Hard. Walker and I instinctively moved our hands toward our guns. Parker stood and opened it without a second thought. Annie stood there holding two take-out bags full of stuff that smelled like taste bud heaven and artery hell.

"Greetings, creeps! I've come bearing gifts!" She stepped in seconds before the sky opened up. Those storm clouds from earlier proved to be far more than just scenery. She set the bags on the table and gave Walker a kiss. "You drinking, Bruce? Am I gonna have to stop you from playing with these boys?"

"Just iced tea, babe."

"Not even from Long Island," I added. Annie set a Styrofoam container in front of each of us and one on

75

the floor for Bukowski.

"Cheeseburgers and fries. Nothing special. Brought the pooch two patties."

"Thanks, babe." Walker kissed her again.

"Yeah, thanks, babe." I winked. Annie flipped me off.

"How'd you know where to find us?" Parker asked.

"You're still in the diner parking lot, dope."

"Ah, right. Whiskey..." He squeezed a packet of ketchup onto his burger and went to town.

"So, how's it going with the investigation?"

"We can't really talk about it," Walker said.

"Meh, it's alright. We might as well. If I can allow Parker to follow us around, I might as well have someone with smarts on the team."

"Hey..." Parker muttered with a full mouth.

"Hey, what? We've already got Scooby Doo and Shaggy. Now we have Daphne."

"Pssh, I'm Velma," Annie scoffed. "Velma's the truly hot one—Daphne's just a slut."

"Ok... then, if we were the JLA, you'd be Wond —"

"—Batman." She beat me to the punch.

"I want to be Batman." Parker frowned. The whiskey had him now.

"Don't talk with your mouth full, Aquaman." Annie smiled. She's a keeper.

"We've established that Zane Bagley was pushed to enact those murders." I said. "It was self-defense nearly each time."

"Nearly?"

"He rammed a woman who was in his way, and she fell over the railing. But she jumped at the very last second. I watched that a few times to make sure. If she didn't, he would have just knocked her down. I'm not saying the guy isn't out of the woods legally speaking, but the evidence all points to self-preservation. Everyone else got stabby due to possession."

"You shitting me?" Annie took a handful of Walker's fries. "Like, demons?"

"Not demons, per-se, no. But evil-as-fuck spirits going for a joy ride in someone else's meat chariot, yes. Places like that have a strong psychic residue that can seep into a person, making them feel sick, or unlike themselves. The Domicile? That place is saturated by horrible crap. It takes psychic influence and jabs a syringe full of adrenaline into its heart. Full-tilt whackadoo.

"And like Travers said, the place grows madness. The worse the murder, the stronger the charge." Parker poured himself more whiskey.

"You *met* Travers?" Annie's jaw dropped. "You guys get to do *all* the fun stuff! What was he like?"

"He's a jibbering nincompoop that's had a ton of time to read a dictionary," I shrugged, then snatched the bottle from Parker. "Anyway, the house was set up for more than just ghosts and goblins. It's balls-deep in the black arts. There's an altar in the basement dedicated to a demon, a room that goes completely bonkers when hit with black light, and then there's the speculum room..."

"The what?" Walker asked.

"Mirror magic. That room with all the mirrors? There were things in those mirrors. Sinister things."

"Ugh! Chills!" Annie pressed against Walker's side.

"What I want to know is who's been taking care of the place? A house that old does not stay in that good of shape. The last renovation was, what, the 1970s? Somebody's been keeping the place from falling down. Parker, I need you to do your thing and get me anything you can on any interactions with that house since Travers. I need to know if the Asylum, or the heritage society or even the damn Girl Scouts had anything do to with it."

"No problem. I'll just use my computer enclave over there, like a certain *caped* crusader."

"Shut up, Aquaman!" I hit him with an unopened mustard packet. Then it occurred to me that there was someone I overlooked. Someone who was there that fateful afternoon and lived to talk about it. "Chuck Gibblin..."

"What?" Walker asked. I stood and grabbed my jacket.

"Come one, Walker. We have to go see Gravenfrost's resident self-proclaimed 'Paranormal Authority' and fast waddler."

"That's weightist," Annie shook her head.

"Is that a thing?"

"Don't be a dick just because someone doesn't fit into the beauty standards set by American media."

"Your husband's built like an underwear model. You don't get to speak." I turned to Walker. "Shall we?" He rose and slid his coat on. He gave Annie a peck on the cheek.

"The computer in the cruiser should be able to pull up his address."

"Good, I'll follow you in case it takes a while. I'll be able to shoot over to Dr. Hobbs's place from there. Don't want to be late for my hot date."

"That reminds me!" Parker stood and ran into his bedroom. He tossed a strip of three condoms at me. "Take three in case you catch a second wind."

"No magnums?" I joked. "Dura-Dink Ultra-Thin. *'Before you shag her, sheathe your dagger.'* Clever slogan."

"Wait, what? Special has a date? There's a haunted house, multiple killings, assorted unspeakable horrors, and *you* have a date?"

"Pretty much, yeah."

"Is this how you normally conduct

78

investigations?"

"Honey-child, if you haven't noticed yet—there's nothing normal about me."

6
FLOGGIN' AND BLOGGIN'
or
THE TAO OF CHUCK
GIBBLIN

The rain came down in sheets. The already
dreary town was drenched like a whimpering dog. Gray,
gray, gray—that's the only color Gravenfrost has heard
of, it seemed. For the rest of New England, this was the
time where the trees start to change into brilliant colors.
The trees here are covered with leaves you pull out of
the rain gutter around your house. I followed Walker's
cruiser past a graveyard that shared property with a
preschool, and the ironic juxtaposition wasn't lost on me
—the beginning and the end with a vacant parking lot
between them. We passed a farmer's market with anti-
supermarket propaganda, and a supermarket with anti-
farmer's market propaganda. The cynic in me wanted to
fire bomb them both. We drove on.

Antique store.
Antique store.

Used books and antiques.

An empty park with swinging swings and seesaws going up and down without needing any help. Fun. We sat at a light and I looked at the folks waiting in an enclosed bus stop across the street. There, sitting between a John Lee Hooker lookalike and a young nurse, sat a man who was a dead ringer for the guy in the cemetery the night before. He looked up and smiled at me. Yeah, that's right. Like he knew I was there and wanted me to see him.

Sonuvabitch!

I flickered my high beams at Walker, then turned the dash strobes on. Not knowing what the hell I was doing, he hit his overheads and stayed put as I arced around him and raced through the intersection. The bus had pulled up and the people filed in. I almost clipped a Volvo as I cut the bus off. I dashed out and slapped the door twice. The driver opened and I was up in a flash— badge out and adrenaline pumping.

"FBI, a moment of your time, please." I panted. "I'm looking for a big fella. Peacoat. Got on the bus right after you, sir." I pointed at John Lee Hooker. I didn't see him anywhere, and a guy that big is hard to miss.

"I was sittin' next to her," John Lee thumbed the nurse a few rows back. "An' I ain't a big dude, less you caught me with my fly open." The bus laughed. I was livid, otherwise I would have laughed too. I checked every seat and nothing. Walker was on the bus now and titled his head toward the door.

"You didn't see anything?" I asked the nurse, who replied by looking at me like she watched me fart in a hat and put it on. "Shit. Sorry for the delay, folks. Thank you for your time and cooperation." Walker stepped off the bus and I slowly followed. I could have sworn I saw that guy clear as day. Maybe the case was getting to me. Maybe I was getting spooked. Maybe—

"Maybe you shouldn't drink during the day," Walker said, NOT finishing my thought. I would *never* think such a thing. He placed his arm across his forehead to block the rain from his eyes.

"I saw that guy last night in the cemetery!" I lit a cigarette, which was no small feat in that rain. "Same guy. I know it."

"He wasn't on the bus, Doyle. You almost caused an accident. This may be your investigation, but it's still my town." He stepped back half a step. I think he may have been bracing for some kind of movie drama where I take a swing at him. If I took a swing at everyone who ever spoke against me, my knuckles would be the size of hubcaps. "You were talking about ghosts and demons all morning. Maybe that's all this was."

"Maybe." I got out of the way of the bus and we made our way to our vehicles. As it passed to take those folks across the bridge to the regular world, I saw the big guy in the middle window, like he'd been there the whole time. Maybe Walker was right, and I was just seeing things. Maybe the town was getting to me. Either way, I was burning lack-of daylight.

*

Our cars stopped in front of a modest suburban home on Marker Street. Really, the only bit of normalcy I've noticed yet. Landscaped lawn, shrubs along the front of the house, a scarecrow holding a "Welcome Y'all!" sign on the door. The rain stopped a half mile back, but the air was still damp and cold. Walker and I walked up the driveway and knocked on the door. A small woman in her seventies opened up with a big smile. All she needed was a tray of cookies and her archetypal design would be complete.

"Hello, Deputy." She grinned. "What brings you out on such a dreary afternoon?"

"Hello, Mrs. Gibblin. This is Federal Agent Doyle—may we come in?" Mrs. Gibblin stood aside to let us through.

"Ma'am," I nodded. The house was refreshingly non-reflective of a place built on ancient burial grounds —polished wood tables and chairs, doilies on every flat surface, and pictures of men in uniform and women smiling on the walls. On the fireplace mantle, a picture of Jesus rested. Even he looked genuinely happy to be there.

"Is everything alright?"

"Yes, Ma'am. We just need to speak with Mr. Charles Gibblin, if that's alright?"

"My husband's been dead for twenty years, I'm afraid. Might you mean Charles Junior?"

"Yes, sorry. Is he around?"

"What's he done?"

"Nothing. Actually, we were hoping he could help us with a case we're investigating. I hear he's the go-to guy for local folklore and that kind of stuff."

"Devil-worshiping poppycock!" she spat. "That boy always had his face in a book about some ghostly gobbledygook, when he should have been learning a trade or joining the Army like his father. He should have been getting his dick wet instead of reading about, whaddayacallem, geckoplasma."

"Ectoplasm..." I corrected her, trying to register if she actually used the words *dick* and *wet*.

"Instead of going outside, he spends his time in the basement looking at those crazy backwards Jap cartoon books with schoolgirls getting schtupped by tentacles. Get a job, I tell him. Meet some people. You know what he says? 'I have over three thousand friends on the Internets.' Can you imagine?"

"Well... he has made a name for himself in certain groups," I tried to salvage poor Chuck's integrity. "A lot of people follow his blog."

"Bloguh! That's not writing. A bunch of smiley faces and videos of cats running amok does not make you Hemingway. *Charles*, I say, go find yourself a nice girl. Do something with your life. I don't sleep well knowing that his ambition doesn't reach past the basement door. What parent wants that? After his father died, God rest his soul, Charles lost all of his whaddayacallem, asspirashins."

"Ah. Well..." Walker was lost.

"Charles around?"

"He's in the basement... he told me not to bother him while he's talking to his girlfriend."

"See? He's found someone," Walker smiled.

"Psshhh... I think it's one of them whaddayacallem, sex hot lines. You know, like 1-800-Drain My Balls, or that sort of thing." Walker and I stood in utter silence.

Shock is a hell of a thing.

Mrs. Gibblin ushered us to the basement door and opened it. A pungent stench like open ass slammed into us.

"Charles! You have visitors!"

"DAMMIT, Mom!" a voice from the fetid deep rang out. "How many times do I have to tell you to not interrupt me when I'm in my lair? Hehhnn..." I elbowed Walker in the arm and emulated jerking off. Walker responded with a *sput-sput* sound. They should give us our own variety show.

"And for the last time, it's Chuck! Charles was my father!"

"Listen to me, you pissy little shit!" Chuck's mom dropped her tone to a growl. "I'll call you whatever the dick I want! And you know why? Because I've babied your ass for forty-two years! And I know—*just know*—that you're waiting for me to die so you can live off the inheritance and not have to do a goddamned thing in this life but get fatter and tug your little dingle like a chimp at the zoo! Now, stop whatever disgusting, useless thing you're doing, and make yourself presentable for these nice police officers! I wish I could convince them to drag you out back and put two in your skull, but I have nothing to bribe them with anymore! Maybe thirty years ago, I could have clamped my vageena around their whaddayacallem, but not now!"

"Th-the police?" Chuck stammered. "Okay..."

"Okay, fellas," Mrs. Gibblin smiled. "Watch your step. Can I get you anything to drink?"

"N-no, thank you... ma'am." Walker said. I stood silent, trying to shake the thought of Mrs. Gibblin going chugga chugga on the meat train.

Each step down to the basement brought a new level of man-funk hell. The first few were a blend of Cheese Doodles and used anal beads, and it only got worse from there. The lair of Chuck Gibblin was exactly what you'd expect a middle-age, Middle Earth, man-child to look like. Computer screens on a large Ikea desk, stacks of comics, piles of clothes, and an inordinate amount of empty tissue boxes. Chuck spun in his swivel chair at the desk with a sickening screech. His face was bright red and he was sweating through his Pearl Jam shirt like he'd just run a marathon... which was unlikely.

"*Hehhnn...* I can assure you that the images on my hard drive are of legal aged women dressed as underage women. It's a... like... uh..." We watched the

85

sweat form under his pits.

"Yes, I am aware of your proclivities, sir, as a member of the FBI." I lied. Screw him. "But we're willing to overlook that if you would aid us in another investigation."

"Y-yeah! Sure! Anything you need!"

"Last week, the cast of *Spook Show* were murdered in the Dickinson house."

"Yeah, I heard. Guess I won't be getting that check." Chuck picked dried salsa off his shirt. At least, I hope it was dried salsa.

"Why'd you leave? Did you know something was going to happen to them?"

"I don't go in there. Nobody should. I was hired to stand out front and tell them what I know. They couldn't pay me enough to set foot in that place. Hell-to-the-no. *Hehhnn...*"

"Don't say that. Grown men should never say that."

"Sorry."

"Okay, so why'd you run?" Walker lifted his foot off of something crunchy, and dry heaved once.

"Something was looking at us. If you would have seen it, you'd have run too! Zane and his flunkies ran toward it, I ran the hell *from* it." He wiped spittle from the corner of his mouth. "You don't go in. Never go in." He was hiding something, but I couldn't peg what. His verbal response was a little too smooth, which betrayed his physical tells. Maybe he didn't want us to find his stash of skunk weed, or blowup doll. Frankly, the evidence has him there for less than five minutes, and Chucky didn't look like a damn shadow assassin. Also, the smell was starting to burn my eyes.

"Am I a suspect or something?"

"No. I'm beginning to think this was a waste of time." I said. "Ready to go, Deputy?"

"About ten minutes ago."

"Thanks for your time, Mr. Gibblin."

"Did you beat him up?" Mrs. Gibblin asked when we made it back upstairs.

"No." Walker smiled.

"Oh..." she frowned. "You know, he was the load I should have swallowed..." Walker and I sprinted out of the house as fast we could.

"*Thankyouforyourcooperationhaveaniceevening!*" I yammered and closed the door behind us.

"I need to douse myself in gasoline and light a Roman candle." Walker shook his shirt out as we stood by the cars.

"Poetic," I lit a cigarette and blew the smoke on myself. "Chuck might be a lot of things, but I don't think he had anything to do with the murders."

"He's got a funky vibe for sure, but he might be half a retard." I love cop lingo. Walker's cellphone rang. He sniffed it before placing it to his face. "Walker. Okay. Since when? Alright, tell the parents I'll be right there. Alright. Where's Sheriff Laidlaw? Oh, he's there too, good. Okay, stand by." He put the phone back in its case.

"Trouble?"

"Three teens are missing. I have to head back to the station."

"Missing? How long?"

"Since 1500 yesterday. Parents came to file a missing persons' report. I have to go."

"Need a hand?"

"No, I can handle it. You have your once-in-a-lifetime date, and I think you might need a shower."

"Good call. Let me know if you change your mind."

"Will do." we shook hands and left Casa De Gibblin with our windows rolled down.

My nose *still* burns.

7
HEAD DOCTOR

Walker's shower idea was a good one. I could feel the Gibblin funk peel off like a second skin, and it also gave the bathtub Susies another look at my meaty clackers. Twice in one day, those lucky devils! Drying off, I walked into the room and looked for Bukowski. I had forgotten that Parker had him for the night. Probably getting his fill of peanut butter and ball hair, the Benedict Arnold. I popped the laptop on and did a search on my gal Lydia—not a long list of stuff, truth be told. Accolades from colleagues and professors. Top of her class. Youngest member of the blah-blah group of accomplished so-and-sos. *Gravenfrost Gazette* had an article about her rise to power at the Asylum. She started as a consultant and wound up top cat. Her angle was traditional ideals with ultra-modern methods. It caught on like crack. She became a zeitgeist in the mental health world. She wanted to keep the State from getting their mitts on the Asylum, like most of the other loony bins across the country. She wanted to "lower the threat of systematic laxation of care and function," whatever that meant. The board of directors got to stay in the big boy chairs, which was aces with them. They gave her free reign.

"I admire the daring innovation of Doctors Oswell and Cattel," she was quoted. "They were unafraid to push the boundaries of medicine and ethics for the common good." Push the boundaries of ethics? I was surprised that got past the editor. Then again, he was probably distracted by the picture of her in that lab coat. She's the woman your daddy secretly wished he bagged instead of your mom. Brains, beauty, drive, ambition, and an ass that could stop traffic. Instead, he had to convince himself that he's satisfied with meatloaf and lackluster blowies once a month.

I just came down hard on your parents, and I apologize.

I brushed my teeth and suited up. GPS said it'd take ten minutes to get to her place even if I hit every red light. If I left now, I'd be on time. I had a reputation to uphold, though, so I decided to pay Mack a visit. I entered the main office, but he was nowhere to be found. *Twin Peaks* was on the tube, and it gave me a strange hyper-awareness. Agent Dale Cooper was one of the main reasons I joined the Bureau. Well, him and Fox Mulder. I rang the bell incessantly until Mack appeared. He burst through the curtain like a magician at an elderly singles bar.

"Tadah! You can stop being a bell-ringing schmuck now! Oh, it's you, my third favorite Fed."

"That's funny, I'm also my third favorite Fed." That wasn't a lie.

"Any top secret tidbits for me today?" Any peculiar happenings you want to bequeef me?"

"Bequeath. And that depends. Got anything a little more date-friendly in the back room?"

"You mean like dick fezzes? I don't use 'em, man. I don't trust 'em."

"I meant wine, and, ew."

"Wine? I look like a liquor store to you now?"

"No. I was at the liquor store already today, and they're much better looking."

"You wound me, sir. One bottle, one question. That's the deal, right?"

"Yep."

"Alright, be right back." He vanished, then reappeared in half the time it took yesterday. "Another Su Room souvenir." He set a bottle of a Californian red wine on the counter. I inspected it, and pretended to know what I was looking at.

"Let me guess, pills and wine?"

"Yeah, she got through half of one bottle before she kicked. Guess whatever pills she took were serious. I'm just glad that it was an overdose. Those are so much easier to clean up after. Just puke, piss and shit on the bed. Easy peasy."

"You are a rare gem, Mack. Say..."

"Yeah?"

"...You ever see or hear about a big guy who lurks in the cemetery by my room? This morning, I swear I saw someone watching me. Then he was gone like—" I snapped my fingers.

"I've never personally seen anyone like that in the boneyard. Haven't heard about it either. Maybe you saw a dude who was visiting his dearly departed?"

"I saw him at a bus stop later on."

"You should have talked to him."

"I tried."

"What happened?"

"He vanished."

"Ghost, then. Don't let it spoil your date." A date I was already five minutes late for.

"Maybe. So, what's your question of the day?"

"Yes! Right! Okay... chem trails..."

"What about them?"

"What the shit are they exactly?"

"You'll find out in a few years," I smiled. "When people start eating each other."

*

Doctor Lydia Hobbs's house was straight out of a 1950s instructional video about how to tell if your neighbor is a filthy Commie. Even the bushes out front were perfectly manicured. I nearly stepped on the lawn, but then Mama Doyle's words popped into my head—*You don't walk across a person's lawn, idiot. That's why God made driveways*! Ah, Ma. I brushed the ash off my lapels and rang the doorbell. Hobbs quickly opened the door and pulled me in by the tie. She wore a form-fitting low cut black dress. Her hair cascaded across her shoulders like chocolate in those commercials.

"You're late, you insufferable man!" she growled. "You are infuriating!"

"I've been told." The interior of the house was Spartan at best: a couch by the bay window with a glass coffee table, a fireplace and a small bar in the living room. That was it. Oh, and a few paintings reminiscent of an Oompa Loompa explosion. Those were the only color-adding items in the white room. She bit her bottom lip seductively and pulled me to the couch.

"Sit." She shoved me down. I held up the wine, which she took from my hand like it was full of hobo piss. "I appreciate the gesture, but neither of us should put this inside us." She set the hobo piss on the coffee table and walked over to the bar just beyond the fireplace.

"Nice place."

"You're a whiskey man, am I right?"

91

"I am." I am.

"I'm a tequila girl, myself." She poured three fingers' worth of whiskey from a fancy crystal decanter. She poured herself a healthy dose of imbibing fluid and swished it lightly. "Though it tends to go straight to my head. Ice?" I shook my head. "Good. I know they say that water sometimes unlocks flavor, but I believe it only dilutes it. If I don't feel the burn sliding down my throat, it's just not worth pouring." She practically floated back to the couch and gave me the drink, which I gulped half in uncharacteristic nervousness. She sat next to me and placed her hand on my lap, which sent tingles to my tinglies.

"I, uh..." I muttered. I was surprised I even got those two sounds to come out. She bit her lip again, and slid her hand up. Her nails matched her lipstick. *Pink Lace*, which was much more naturally seductive than your typical red. She was throwing me for a loop, which was not like me. There was something about her that knocked me off my game.

"Hope you don't mind." She smiled. I shook my head like a simpleton and downed the rest of my drink. She set our glasses down and straddled me. Her dress hiked up so high I could damn-near see the Promised Land. We began to kiss like we were in a pie eating contest. "You—mm—insufferable—man," she stated between the lip smacks. "I—MMmf—find nothing— mmm—more infuriating and—mmm—fucking hotter than a man—mm—who doesn't know his place." She pulled back and began unbuckling my belt. I grabbed her hips and pulled her onto the bulge she caused, and looked into her dark eyes.

"I'm my own man, baby." She slid off and slowly slid her dress down. She stood in nothing but shear black panties, and I didn't know which god to thank for that, so I thanked them all. She plucked my glass off the table and swayed those mind erasing hips back to the bar for a refill. She handed me the drink and stared at me with both lust and contempt.

"I'm used to being subjected to sniveling, spineless boys who *think* they're men. Pathetic! But you... you're just so fucking arrogant and headstrong. You better not be all talk, Agent." I motioned to my junk that was ready to puncture the ceiling and smiled.

"That look spineless to you, Doc?" She returned the smile, and pushed the table out of the way. She sank to her knees, removed my drawers, and showed me why her title was Head Doctor.

What?

You want to strike that from the official document? Hell no! I formally protest! I'm giving credit where credit's due. Fine—I'll skip aHEAD. See what I did there? Just for the record, when you ask someone for details, expect details, maybe.

Fine.
Fine!

An hour later, that's right, an *hour,* Hobbs dismounted and reclined on the couch like she was posing for a painting. She took her glass and emptied it with a gulp.

"That work for you?" I panted.

"Oh, you'll do just fine," she laughed softly. "Be a good boy, and fill me up?"

"Gonna need a half hour and a ham sandwich if you... oh, you mean your drink?" I laughed. Been a while since I had a good buzz. Been even longer for a good lay. I pulled my drawers and pants up and staggered to the bar. I figured it was my empty stomach mixing with the top shelf hooch that set my head to spin cycle. As I poured her drink half in the glass and half on the carpet, a strange thought occurred to me. "Wait. I'll *do* just fine? I thought I *did* just fine?"

"Figure of speech, Agent." Hobbs began to play with herself. "I expect there will be much more *doing*."

"Yesh, you put it that way..." Man, I couldn't think worth a damn. I nearly fell into the bar, but caught myself. "Whoop, sorry." My phone rang in my pocket. I managed to slide my hand in on the fourth try. Hobbs moaned as she moved her hand between her legs, getting back into the swing of things. Whoever was calling me better make it quick.

"Cheh?"

"Doyle?" It was Parker. He sounded worried.

"Cheh."

"Thank God! Listen, you have to get out of Hobbs's house! Now!" She was really going to town on herself now, which was by far more interesting than whatever whatshisface was saying. She let out another moan to indicate that I was missing out on round two.

"Okay, thangs for call..."

"It's *her*, dammit!" Parker shouted. The room began to spin. That was some whammo whiskey, man. "*She* bought the house! *She* called Bagley a failure! The audio from the Asylum—"

"We haven't had dinner..." I muttered. "I ate out, but—CHEE-HEE HEEEEee!" I snorted.

"The hell is wrong with you? Walker and I are on our way! We—" I dropped my phone. My fingers were on strike. I looked to Hobbs, who was suddenly dressed.

"You might as well do it," she said. "I didn't realize his tolerance would be this strong."

"Whuh?" I asked.

"I wasn't talking to you, Agent Doyle." I heard the sharp *TINK* of some poor bastard getting hit upside the head with a metal baseball bat. As the carpet rushed up to greet my face, I knew it was me.

8
SPECIAL DELIVERY

"I cannot *believe* you made me drag him to the car!" Lydia Hobbs shouted. I was wedged on the floor in the back of a speeding car—zip tied at the ankles and wrists—duct tape over my mouth. I was surprised they didn't shove me in the trunk. "And slow down! We don't need to be pulled over, idiot!"

"Sorry, Mistress... but he weighed a ton." said her companion. I knew that voice.

Waifly.

"And yet *I* managed just fine, you fraction of a man!"

"Sorry, Mistress..." I heard sirens. Hobbs sank in her seat so she wouldn't be recognized. The sirens zipped past, heading to her house no doubt.

"You will clean my boots later."

"Yes, Mistress."

"With your tongue."

"Of course, Mistress."

"MmmMFF MMM!" I said. Hobbs looked down

at me and ran her fingers through my hair.

"Our Thaumaturgy is awake," she smiled.

"I still don't see why *he* of all people is our—"

"—You don't have to see anything, slug! Just do as I command!"

"Yes, Mistress..." that little rat fucker deliberately hit a pothole, causing my head to bounce hard against the floor.

"UuuUUR!" I shouted. My head was still in free fall from the mickey she slipped me and the kiss with the bat. I wanted to vomit, but talked myself out of it. Vomit + taped mouth = reroute. Nobody wants that.

"I'm surprised that you're awake," Hobbs began. "You have quite the tolerance for drugs and alcohol. Your liver is either superhuman or no longer in your body." I wanted to tell her something witty and profound. I also wanted to tell her to eat a bag of dicks.

"Mrff," was as close as I could get.

"Don't worry, we'll be home shortly. Once we get you inside, I promise we will make it quick. Then we can get back to what we were doing earlier, eh?" She licked her upper lip. Waifly let out a pathetic growl. "You can watch again, Jeremy."

"Thank you, Mistress."

Gross.

The car stopped and I heard the sound of a gate opening. We drove up the driveway and parked. The back door opened and I was pulled out by someone in a black body stocking that smelled like mold and dog farts.

Son of a bitch.

"We meet again! *Hehhnn*!" Chuck laughed like a poorly-scripted comic book villain. He hoisted me up as Waifly grabbed my legs. I pulled them close then shoved him to the ground. Chuck and I both laughed. Waifly pulled my gun from his belt and pressed it to my cheek.

"You aren't worthy." he growled.

"Jeremy." Hobbs sounded like a school teacher who was sick of the bullshit. "Cut his feet free so he can walk, and put that gun away before I make you use your colon as a holster. Quickly, gentlemen!" Chuck gave me a good jostle after Waifly cut the zip ties around my ankles and handed the knife to his boss. A few shoves later, I was standing in the grand foyer of the goddamned Devil's Domicile. Maybe it was the drugs, but I saw people lining up around the room, up the stairs, and down the hallways. I would have waved, but my hands were still behind my back.

"What's he lookin' at? Chuck asked.

"He's seeing the spirits!" Hobbs said with excitement. "Tell me, what do you see?" she ripped the tape off my mouth with a hearty tug.

"YOU! OW! *FUCK!*" That really hurt like a bitch. "I'm seeing a bunch of shit zippers that are going to rot in prison! You set Zane and his crew up, didn't you! You and your two stenchmen here, who are complete idiots that only want to sniff your smelly goody hole!" I was clearly still reeling from the drugs. "They died because of what?"

"They died because of chaos." Hobbs's eyes flared. She was bat-guano crazy.

Always my luck.

"Bring him to the Reflection Room. Jeremy, prepare for our other guests. I'm certain once they search my house, they'll be along." Waifly nodded and ran toward the basement. Chuck poked my spine with what I hoped was my backup revolver, and ushered me toward the stairs. I walked between the wall and a row of mutilated ghosts. Inmates, cultists, victims all came out to see the new guy. Some smiled, some laughed without sound, but most looked sad. We hooked a left at the top of the stairs and I looked over the balcony at a sea of dead faces staring back. My vision spun like a drunk uncle at a wedding.

"He does see them, Mistress!" Chuck exclaimed.

"That's why he's perfect. The other one was a fake. Nice abs, but a fake."

"You're perfect too," I said. She genuinely smiled. "Like, physically perfect—but your brain is all cake town." She genuinely frowned. Cake town is apparently my word for crazy when I'm seeing triple. Which I was.

"Let me tell you what we will accomplish tonight," she began. "I am a follower of the Dickinson Doctrine, that is to say, that evil and chaos can be cultivated and shaped to one's own desire. This house proves his containment theory. Now I want to take it to the next level."

"A Tupperware party?"

"A party, yes. You will be possessed by as many spirits as possible, then you and I will make a child."

"A bit much for a first date, don't you think? And I'm not much of a role model."

"You are just the conduit. You will sire a child of pure chaos—a living embodiment of Dickinson's legacy!"

"If you just need a turkey baster, why not have Chubby Chuckers here do it?"

"Ew, please." She grimaced.

"Aw..." poor Chuck said.

"I tried, buddy. Back to the Kleenex." He slammed me against the room door. "Hey, before I forget—your mom really fucking hates you, man. That, and she totally wants to gobble my nob like a heron choking down a fish." I simulated gagging sounds—*guk-guk-guk*—and Chuck aimed the revolver at my head. Hobbs pushed his hand aside.

"Go help Jeremy prepare!" she ordered. "And make sure Deputy Walker's surprise is ready. If heroics overpower the trauma he associates with this house, I'm sure it'll ruin his day! We've planned this over and over. Go!"

"What are you talking about, you bitch?!" I shouted. She turned the doorknob and I tumbled backwards into the mirror room.

"Make it quick!" she ordered the room then slammed the door. I scrambled to my feet. I wasn't going to let Hobbs and the douche squad win. I rammed the door and fell on my ass like an idiot.

Maybe I *was* going to let them win.

I sat up and tried to clear my head. A candle was lit on each wall, and their flames danced and flickered. Focus on the flames, I thought. Shapes and shadows began to form in the mirrors.

"Hey, fellas," I greeted the shapes. "Listen, the last guy who was here got a blow job. You think you could arrange something for me?"

"Doyle..." one of the mirrors said.

"Yeah?"

"C'mere."

"Okay." I stood and approached the mirror to the right of the door, because, why not? The shadow sharpened into a familiar face. "Hey, Dad."

"I'm disappointed in you, boy."

"No you aren't. My father isn't dead. I know you aren't him, so cut the shit." The face changed to a man who'd been burned alive. "Nice special effects."

"Bobby..." the man said through ashen lips.

"Mr. Clarmont." I acknowledged my childhood neighbor, who was, in fact, dead.

"You let me die, Bobby."

"Did I? I had something to do with the fateful night you drank yourself to sleep with a lit cigar? I had something to do with that other than wishing your spank mags survived the fire? *EEEENT!* Try again, house! Try harder! Can't do it, can you? Not prepared to face a true-blue badass *muthafucka*, are you!"

"Doyle..." the mirror on the floor said. The glass warped and pushed out. A man rose up and looked at me with a mix of anger and profound sadness. The room became a tilt-o-whirl as the other mirrors chattered like cicadas, then *BANG*—stone still and silent. "Doyle... how could you do this, man?" Tony Liu said. Smoke billowed from his mouth and from the hole under his jaw... where I had shot him. His left eye was a black, oozing hole. The room began to crack and tear violently —chunks fell away and revealed a place I've tried very hard to forget. I could smell the rain against the pavement. I could see the lanterns hanging over the window of The Jade Garden restaurant. *Ah, hell...* I thought.

I'm in Chinatown again.

9
朋友们不要让朋友拍的朋友在头上

[FRIENDS DON'T LET FRIENDS SHOOT FRIENDS IN THE HEAD]

"You ready to do this?" Tony asked. We sat across the street from the Jade Garden restaurant, in an unassuming black van that only slightly screamed FEDERAL-TYPES INSIDE.

"We're supposed to wait for backup." I replied. "So, sure."

"My cracker," he smiled.

"No. You don't have the pigmentation to say things like that." I lit a cigarette. "I can say things like *'You're my favorite bowl of rice,'* or, *'It's not windy in this van, why are you squinting?'* Because whites are inherently racist. At least, that's what my Uncle Al says."

"Uncle Al?"

"Sharpton."

"I sit corrected," Tony laughed and drummed the

steering wheel. We had been building a case on Li Xian, owner of the restaurant, for damn near a year. You see, Xian was a mid-level mucky muck in The Dragon Cult, which only *sounds* like an awesome '80s hairband. The Dragon Cult has been around long before Marco Polo ever heard of a chopstick. They profit off the vices of mankind, as well as corruption. Traditionalists believe the Cultists have supernatural powers, but from what I've witnessed, unless human trafficking and sex-slave trade are super powers, these guys are as supernatural as bubblegum. But they are dangerous, make no mistake, and very well organized. Nobody in their right minds would dare go up against the DC.

Lucky for them, me and Tony left our right minds back at the Bureau.

The rain had let up to a piss sprinkle and I could smell the concrete-and-funk of the city. The lanterns out front buzzed a threat of spontaneous combustion as we entered the restaurant. The tired-looking hostess smiled at us and grabbed two menus.

"Good evening. Table for two?"

"Three, actually," I said.

"Yes, we have a reserved private table with Li Xian," Tony added. Her smile faded into a thin line as we showed our badges.

"I'm sorry, but—" Tony silenced her with a raised hand.

"Sweetie, I'm all out of give a damn," he said. She grabbed his arm and grumbled.

"叛徒. 你是白人的狗."

"I'm from Philly. You can save that motherland bullshit." We walked to the kitchen where a handful of cooks darted around like hummingbirds, deep frying this, woking that, pouring viscous sugar goop on the neighborhood cats.

"What did she say?"

"Nothing. Just called me a traitor and the white man's dog. No big." I knocked on the door marked employees only, and was greeted by a string of angry Cantonese... or Mandarin. I'm ignorant.

"What?"

"He told us to go find a little boy to have ass relations with," Tony translated.

"Guess he's busy. Maybe we should come back another time?"

"That'd be the polite thing to do," Tony nodded and kicked the door down. I expected goons, maybe a few ninjas or something, but no, Li Xian sat alone at his desk and puffed a long pipe. The room was full of smoke like someone set off a fog machine, and it smelled like roasted anus.

"I expect the Bureau will compensate me for the door?" Xian said, and folded the newspaper he'd been reading.

"Federal Agents Liu and Doyle. You are under arrest for the charges of human trafficking and slave trade." Tony waved the smoke from his face.

"Among other things," I added. "I don't know what kind of ragweed you're smoking, pal, but it stinks like hot garbage."

"This is an experimental neural toxin we've been perfecting," Xian puffed harder. "The smoke plays with the mind, you see. Twists it, unravels it—brings forth madness."

"Bullshit!" Tony spat. "You'd be affected too. Doyle, get the cuffs on that fool." I dangled my handcuffs like a hypnotist's watch and shook the fuzz that was forming in my head.

"Man, you come right out of a comic book," I said. I've always wanted to say that in context. If you don't know what movie that's from, then I can't help you.

104

Xian wheezed out a laugh. His eyes turned the color of vitamin pee, and he spouted a string of words only Tony could understand. I managed to cuff one of his hands while Tony began to look like someone punched him in the gut. A quick head slam to the desk caused Xian to shut the hell up. "You're under arrest, dick skin."

"Sit him up, let me put a bullet in him," Tony growled. I looked toward the kitchen and saw the cooks closing in. Their eyes were glowing like Xian's were.

"T! Behind you, man!" I shouted. Tony spun to see the knife-and-cleaver-wielding cooks. He aimed his gun at the lead.

"Back up! Stop where you are!" They kept coming. Tony blasted the lead in the chest, sending him scrambling back. The other cooks caught him and straightened him back up like nothing happened.

"Yessssssss..." Xian laughed. "You are desperately out of your league, gentlemen." His face looked like a lizard's, scaly and grayish-green. His smile exposed a row of dagger teeth and a flicking tongue. Tony planted a bullet in the cook's dome, and he dropped.

"Hell," I darted to the door, and helped him put the zombie cooks down. I looked to my partner, but he no longer looked like Tony Liu. He, too had eyes like amber. His jaw extended low—unhinged and sinewy.

"T?" He looked at me with those monster eyes and shouted like a man possessed. Next thing I knew I was sent flying across a kitchen range, knocking pots of boiling water and God knows what all over. Tony wrenched a fillet knife from the grip of a dead cook and stalked his way closer.

"Stop! The hell are you doing?" I shouted, but my voice also sounded strange. I raised my gun and saw my hand was rotted and covered with maggots. I didn't even see Tony rush in to tackle me through the swinging doors to the dining area. The place was a ghost town once the shooting started, so it was just me and my friend, two monsters trying to kill each other. Tony straddled me with the knife hovering over my chest. I gripped his hands in mine and struggled to keep the knife from getting any closer. I punched at his fanged mouth without leverage. He laughed and bore down. My gun was just out of reach. Might as well been on the moon. The thin knife point touched my coat, pierced it, and then slowly entered my left pectoral muscle. Sirens in the distance meant backup would arrive just in time to zip up my body bag. In a last ditch effort, I went for my gun. I was able to finger the grip enough to pull it closer. I grabbed it and jammed it under Tony's jaw and fired. The bullet entered, took a right at Albuquerque, and exited through his left eye. Tony fell on top of me and we just laid there bleeding into the carpet. The NYPD arrived the same time our backup did, and quickly secured the area.

I went to the hospital.
Tony went to the morgue.
Xian was nowhere to be found.

The toxicology report showed that me, Tony, and those cooks were exposed to an extremely powerful hallucinogen. They said it was most likely military-grade. My supervisor, Bradly Ross, said it was a minor miracle I was able to come down from the effects. Xian was planning to sell the chemical to terrorists to use in major metropolitan areas. The destruction would be catastrophic. Xian had the lab and was holding several captives in the basement of the restaurant. Turned out the human trafficking was for test subjects. We were able to shut the place down and confiscate the crap he'd already developed. Even though Xian was still out there with the formula, the Bureau saw this as a win for the good guys. Good for them. My partner was still dead.

And I killed him.

      I was sent to rehab for a while. Therapy and whatnot. *It wasn't your fault*, they said. *He was trying to kill you too.* Lip service to cover up what they were really thinking: Partner killer. Failure. After a while, I was back on cases. No partner, though—nobody wanted to step up and try their luck. That suited me fine. The nature of the investigations changed as well. I was no longer sent to the big crime stuff. Instead, I was tossed all the weird shit nobody knew what to do with. I was more than happy to chase down chupacabras and UFO conspirators. Hell, just made me feel more like my hero Spooky Mulder.

      "I had a wife! Two baby girls at home, you shit!" Tony roared. The fiery smoke curled around his head like a devil's halo. "You had nothing! You are nothing!"

      "What did you want me to do, T?" I pleaded. "You were trying to kill me too!" He pointed an accusatory finger like the hand of fate.

      "You should have let me!" I dropped to my knees. Spirits stood around me and spoke in unison. Screams and sobs and laughter blended into an overwhelming white noise with a high-pitch squeal to spice it up. The cotton in my head was torn away, red and pulpy, revealing the raw nerve beneath. The pressure was more than I could handle.

      "You're right, T," I admitted. "I am nothing..." the candles blew out, and it was over. Hobbs opened the door, and the room was the room again.

      "Agent Doyle?" she whispered. I drew a deep breath and let it leak out slowly.

      "He's not here."

10
HOUSE OF SHARDS

"Hurry and untie us, woman!" I ordered. My voice was twisted and graveled, like Buddy Holly singing through an earthquake. "We must begin before those cretins or the heroes interfere!" Hobbs rushed in and cut the zip tie with the knife Waifly had handed over earlier.

"Where should we?" She asked. Her eyes were wide with a blend of terror and sheer excitement.

"The master bedroom," I said. "Take us there." Hobbs took my hand and guided me down the hall, to the right of the mirror room.

"They're here!" I heard Chuck shout from the other side of the house. The Calvary. Too little, too late.

*

ARD: THIS NEXT BIT WAS RELAYED TO ME BY MY COHORTS.
ARR: WHY WOULD I CARE WHO IT WAS RELAYED BY?
ARD: BECAUSE, THIS WHOLE THING'S BEEN A FIRST PERSON NARRATIVE. TO SUDDENLY

JUMP TO FIRST PERSON OMNISCIENT WOULD
BE BAD FORM.
ARR: GOD, YOU ARE SO WEIRD.
ARD: YEAH...

Walker's squad car jumped the curb as he
screeched to a halt. Parker jumped out with his revolver
at the ready, and ran to the door. Walker removed his
shotgun from the trunk and froze halfway up the
driveway. Parker tried the door, but it was locked. He
looked back at Walker and tried to wave him over.

"Come on, Bruce!" He urged. "Doyle needs us!"
"I-I don't know if I... can." Walker stammered.
Parker moved to his friend and placed a reassuring hand
on his shoulder.

"Time to step up, Deputy. Time to show this
place that it's got nothing on you. Now's your chance for
some get-back!" Parker gave his shoulder a squeeze and
returned to the door, this time with Walker right behind.
Walker took a deep breath and aimed the shotgun at the
doorknob.

"Stand back," he ordered. Parker moved and
Walker blew a basketball-size hole where the knob used
to be. He kicked the door open, rushed in, and was
greeted by a series of gunshots that tore the door frame
to his right. He fired up the stairs at the sack of crap in
the body stocking, sending shards of wall everywhere.

"SHIT!" Chuck yelped and retreated back into
the hallway. Waifly shrieked from the kitchen and ran to
the basement stairs.

"Parker, take the imp! I'll head up!" Walker
stalked up the stairs. Parker nodded and made his way
toward the kitchen. He paused at the doorway leading
down and flicked on the light switch. Nothing.

"Jeremy," Parker called out. "If you're down
there, please surrender and come up. Don't make me
come down there. I've been hunted by mob hit men for

the last three years, and I'm still here. What does that tell you? I have a gun, too. Do you? You any good at using it? Me, I'm a crack shot. I could shoot your dick off from half a mile away. But I'm not going to—no sir. If you don't come up, I'm gonna head down there and pistol-whip the bitch right out of you! You hear me, Jeremy?" Silence. Parker thought he heard whimpering, but he couldn't be sure. Then a male's voice screamed out.

"Help me! Please!" *That wasn't Jeremy*, Parker thought.

"Hello?"

"Help me, man! This freaky little guy has me tied to this altar thing! He had me gagged!"

"What's your name?"

"Help me, for God's sake!" The voice was panicked. Sounded like a teenager. "He's got a gun, man!"

"Shit," Parker muttered. Could be a trap, could be one of the missing teens. Maybe they were in on it? So many variables, so little time. If the kid was hurt or killed and Parker let it happen, he wouldn't be able to live with it. He cocked the hammer on his revolver and took the first step down.

*

Lydia Hobbs removed her dress with what the homies call the quickness, and once again I was looking at milk white skin so sexy it would've given the Nestle's rabbit an aneurysm. She spread herself on the large bed, then looked startled.

"Those were gunshots!" she gasped. "Hurry! We have to hurry!" I lifted her knife and started cutting the bed sheet into lengths. "What...what are you doing?" I began to tie her arms and legs to the bed posts. "I won't fight! I want this! Look how wet I am!" I did. She was.

"Must restrain you. Once our... ghost dick is inside you, the pain may be unbearable. The chaos will be intense but short. We cannot have you struggling, or breaking the ritual." I finished tying her down and kissed her. "Now for the screams..." I held one last piece of fabric. She opened her mouth and willingly let me gag her. She was a true believer in the power. I stood next to the bed and took one last look. I raised my hands and began the ritual.

"Oh, chaos! Oh, swirling madness! Let our demon seed burrow deep into the verdant and fragrant nappy dugout before us!"

"Mmff?"

"Shh, don't interrupt the ritual. Oy and vey! Warriors come out to play*eey*ay! Let us impale her with meaty righteousness and bring forth a new Age of Aquarius! And... I... oh, I lost the flow." I touched her nose. "*Boop*! The ritual is now fruityliscious!" I could see by the look in her eyes that Mistress Lydia Hobbs was terribly confused.

"I can't believe you fell for that shit," I laughed. "I thought I blew it when I said 'ghost dick'! Don't look so angry, baby. You had no idea who you were dealing with. When it comes to monsters and demons and haunted taco stands, *I'm* the guy the big boys send to take care of it. You royally screwed the pooch, by the way. I had zero reason to implement you in the murders. You could have waited till this whole thing blew over, and tried again. *Tsk!* Typical rookie mistake. Sit tight, hot stuff. Once this is over, I'll be back with a nice pair of handcuffs and criminal charges." I walked to the door with her knife. I didn't have my guns, and who knew if the stenchmen got the drop on my boys. Then something occurred to me. I walked back to the bed and draped the comforter over Hobbs. It was a bit chilly after all.

"Never let it be said that Bobby Doyle isn't a gentleman."

*

Walker peeked around the top of the stairwell wall. The hallway was pitch black and seemingly empty save for a light coming from a room halfway down. The screaming in his head grew louder. *That room*, he thought. Each step made his stomach tighten. Chuck knew which room to choose as his Alamo. That wasn't coincidence, Walker knew. Hobbs must have read the file and used it against him.

"Charles Gibblin Jr., come out with your hands up!" Walker shouted. "You will have only one chance to end this without being turned into chopped meat!" Two sets of whimpering sounds sent shivers up his spine, followed by Chuck whispering *shut up!* harshly. Walker swung the door wide and froze.

On the bed a teenage boy and girl sat, exactly where Walker's brother Matt and his girlfriend did years ago. The boy held a trembling gun to the girl's temple. Chuck stood on the other side of the bed and smiled.

"*Hehhnn...* kind of brings you back, doesn't it, Deputy?"

"Put the guns down, the both of you!" Walker demanded. The teenager's hand began to drop until Chuck jammed his own gun against the back of his head.

"No, Seth, you listen to me, not him. Got it?!" Chuck growled.

"H-help us, s-sir." Seth pleaded.

"I want you to put your shotgun down, pig. Toss it down the hall, and brace yourself for an historical reenactment!" Walker set the safety on and tossed it. Chuck pointed his gun back to Walker and picked his nose. "You must be full of fear, eh? Scared stiff? You're gonna watch 'Matthew' here blow his little girlfriend's head off, then I'm gonna shoot you. How's that sound?"

"Seth, do not pull that trigger."

"Seth, it's the only way you'll make it out alive. *Hehhnn.* No cooze is worth your life, Seth. Even one as cute as Jess, here."

"That's coming from a pathetic scumbag who's about to die for a woman who wouldn't even let him sniff her chair when she got up. I wouldn't listen to him." Walker forced a laugh to piss Chuck off. Truth was, the fear was creeping throughout his limbs. His trauma was no longer a scab, but a gushing wound. But there was one thing inside him that fought back against the terror.

Redemption.

"Shut up, pig!" Chuck screamed. "Once this is over, we'll—"

"Do nothing, dipshit loser. You think a fox like Hobbs wants to do anything with a hog like you, other than use you for fodder? Come on, Charles! Even you can't be that stupid!"

"For the last time, it's CHUCK!" He started to pull the trigger. *That's alright*, Walker thought. *He takes me out, and maybe Seth takes him out. Fare trade.* Seth dropped the gun to the floor—Chuck's eyes followed in absolute rage—Walker quick-drew his sidearm and planted a round in Chuck's forehead. Brains slapped the wall behind him like a watermelon at a Gallagher concert. Seth and Jess gripped each other tightly.

"You two alright?" Walker lowered his weapon. The teens nodded frantically. "Follow me, we'll get you out of here." They followed. I ran into the three of them near the balcony. Walker tossed me my confiscated backup piece.

"The missing teens?" I asked. Walker nodded. "Where's the third?"

"The buh-buh-basement," Jess said. "Oh my God! Patrick's still down there!"

"Our friend Parker is down there now." Walker ushered the kids down the steps.

"I'll back him up!" I said. "You get them outside."

*

"Jeremy... come out with your hands up. I've seen the footage, Jer, I know where you're hiding." Once Parker hit the last step, he spun to catch the blind spot behind the stairs where Andrew had ambushed Zane. This time, however, the spot was empty. Parker tried the light switch at the bottom with the same results.

"He's deeper in, man..." the voice in the dark warbled.

"Thanks," Parker acknowledged.

"They took me, Seth, and Jess... freaking *snatched* us, man..."

"You must be Patrick, then. I need you to keep quiet, Pat. I'll get you out."

"Thirty six... thirty six..." Waifly's voice floated from the far side of the basement. Parker couldn't get a bead on him.

"You're too smart for this, Jer. Hobbs is just using you." Parker pulled his cellphone out and used the screen as a flashlight. Risky, but what are you gonna do? He made out a shape hogtied to the altar on his knees. His head hovered over a silver bowl. Patrick's eyes grew wide with terrified hope in the green light. "A sacrifice, Jer? A little Dark Ages, don't you think? You've played this all wrong, man. She just using you like a pawn. You should have told her to go to hell, when she tried to enlist you. It'd be *you* running the Asylum, Jer. Give yourself up—show her you're your own man!" Waifly bounded screaming from the murk and fired. The recoil

114

from my Beretta M9 caused it to jump back and crack Waifly in the forehead. The support beam above Parker's head sprinkled bits of wood. Parker lunged, grabbed Waifly by the arm, and kept true to his promise of pistol-whipping the bitch out of him.

"What's that sound?" I asked, bounding down the steps. "Sounds like someone using a hammer on a squeak toy."

"Over here, Doyle!" Parker panted. "Free the poor bastard tied to the altar, would you?" I obeyed the gun-swinging, lunatic journalist.

"You ready to go, Marcellus Wallace?" I asked the kid as I untied him.

"Wh-who?"

"I'm going to tie you back up for Asmodeus."

"That a diarrhea medicine?"

"Ha! You hear that?" I shouted at the blood sigil, "You're a loose stool remedy!"

"You feeling alright, Doyle?" Parker asked.

"Nope!" I nodded. Truth was, I was still reeling from the dead man radio station in my skull.

"Whuh-where's Mistress?" Waifly muttered through his mangled mouth.

"She's tied up on a house call." I ushered Patrick up the stairs.

"That was terrible," Parker shook his head. He kicked Waifly in the balls, then the midsection. When he was good and fetal, Parker recovered my Beretta and handed it over. I emptied the magazine into the sigil of Asmodeus for good measure.

"Been a long night." I helped Parker drag Waifly up the stairs. Sheriff Laidlaw and the other deputies finally arrived to the party. Walker met us in the foyer, a look of stoic relief on his face. The Three Pendéjos win again. I directed the officers up the stairs to collect Nutty McHotpants. They were in for a treat.

"What in the sweet hell went on here?" Laidlaw

scratched his chin.

"What went on, Sheriff, is that your boy Walker here not only found three kidnapped teenagers, he also saved the life of a federal agent and apprehended the shit-crusted perineums behind a ritualized multiple homicide." I smiled. Walker opened his mouth to interject, but I word-blocked him. "And this guy helped too, I guess." I thumbed at Parker.

"I'll be..." Laidlaw set his hands on his hips, trying to process the information.

"My suggestion to you, Sheriff, is that you either give him a dramatic bump in pay, or just retire and let him take over. Because, let's face it, you make a better tree stump than lawman these days."

"Asshole," Laidlaw spat. A string of foul language erupted from the second floor as two deputies practically dragged a bedsheet-wrapped Hobbs downstairs.

"Help me! I beseech you!" she screamed to the house. She caught sight of Waifly and screamed some more. "You failed me! You pathetic piece of—"

"Actually, princess, Jeremy here fought like a warrior for your honor," Parker said. "Isn't that right?" Waifly coughed a tooth out and nodded. Another deputy cuffed him and walked him out. I stopped the guys from taking Hobbs outside.

"Hold up. I have to ask just one thing: What were we going to have?"

"Wh-what?" she seethed.

"To eat. You invited me over for dinner."

"You idiot. I wasn't going to feed you."

"Tsk! Terrible hosting etiquette! Didn't stop *you* from getting a mouthful, though." I winked and waved them on. She shouted all kinds of fun stuff as they tossed her in the squad car. Next stop, the hotel county lockup.

Such a lovely place.

Such a lovely fa—ugh, The Eagles suck.

We walked outside and I felt the pull of the house trying to coax me back. Parker exhaled as if he was holding it for hours.

"Well, we did it." He smiled and slapped Walker on the back. "I'm proud of you, man. You took care of business."

"You both did," I agreed.

"You didn't have to lie to Laidlaw, Doyle." Walker stated.

"Who said I did? You guys came to the realization that I was porking a psychotic malcontent, then pulled my ass out of the fire."

"Didn't look like you needed help," Parker said. We walked to the curb and I patted my pants for cigarettes. No such luck.

"I played the odds and figured her zealousness would overpower any need to call my bluff. For what it's worth, the ghastholes inside really tried their best. They did a pretty good number on me."

"Now what?" asked Parker.

"Now we lock it up until the county coroner comes to take Chuck's dead ass to the morgue." Walker spat on the driveway.

"No. Now what we do is three things," I began. "One: go get my car and coat from Hobbs's joint and bring them to me here. Two: one of you is going to get me some food, two bottles of Graves End, and three packs of Mal Burro cigs. Three: you'll leave me alone."

"What? The hell are you talking about?" Walker frowned.

"I'm staying. This place is a sickness, and I'm the freelance gynecologist. Or whatever. I'm so hungry. While you do my bidding, I'm going to prepare myself, then, I'm going to spend the rest of the night figuring out a way to pop this pimple from the ass of the world."

"Did you just call my hometown the ass of the world?"

"Shh... hungry. Go do my bidding, minions!"

"I'll get your stuff from Hobbs's, as it's an active crime scene," Walker shrugged.

"You like Bingo Bango Burger?" Parker asked. I began to salivate.

"Hell yeah I do! I didn't know this place has America's most whimsical burger joint! Make sure you get the extra-whammy-size Bingo Bango Fries. And as many salt packets as you can steal." They took off, eager to please their master. I sat against the fence and picked through a few of the cursing stones. Some of them have been there for decades. I wondered if any of the poor bastards on the rocks met untimely deaths, debilitating sickness, or just bad gas. Faces in the windows glared with hatred, or stared without hope, as the time ticked away. I meditated, pushed the protective white light through my body like a vaccine, and hoped it would be enough to fend off anything the house threw at me.

*

Walker returned first, and handed me my coat and tie.

"This is a bad move," he said, as he handed me my cellphone after I finished pulling my tie tight.

"Duly noted. Fact of the matter is I may be able to set these souls free and put this whole thing to bed for good. Worth a shot, right? If it goes tits-up and they kill me, I become a ghost and *really* annoy the hell out of them." I lit one of my remaining cigs, and it felt like Thanksgiving and Christmas at the same time. Thanksgivemas. Parker arrived and hustled over.

"Sorry, there was a wait at Bingo Bango. The Caretaker was holding up the drive through. He was on, like, a moped."

"The who what now?" I snatched the greasy bag of yum from Parker's hands.

"The Caretaker. He's a local nut who dresses up as some third-rate superhero and runs around trying to help people. His arch nemesis is another butthead called The Gravedigger. I think it's a sex thing." Walker rubbed his forehead.

"The guy's named after the omelette? I take it back, Gravenfrost isn't the ass of the world." I nodded.

"*Thank* you!" Walker smiled.

"It's the taint."

"If you weren't about to get your asshole torn through your mouth by a house full of ghosts, I'd punch you."

"What's our next move?" Parker brought us back to task.

"You guys split the scene, I go in and eat. Try to get a handle on how to create a mass exorcism, or something."

"We'll wait here." Walker said. I shook my head and stamped out my cig.

"Negative. There's nothing you can do. Walker, you have a hot wife to get back to and a shit-ton of paperwork—and Parker has to feed Bukowski."

"He's too good for you, you know." Parker smiled.

"Story of my life. I don't make it out, he's yours."

"The coroners get Chuck's body out?" Walker asked.

"Honestly? I don't know. I think so. I was in a deep meditation with ghosts and drugs buzzing in my head like a beehive. The entire cast of *Good Times* could have gone in there for I know." I shook their hands and moseyed to the door. I took one deep breath and stepped in.

Everyone came out to play now. The house made the cover to Sgt. Pepper's look like the line for a gas station restroom. I dragged a big dusty leather club chair from the den to the foyer, and a candelabra with four candles. I poured some whiskey in a circle big enough for me to stretch my legs, then sprinkled in packet after packet of salt, while imbuing the circle with as much positive energy as possible. Once the circle was complete, I sat, took a swig, and lit one of the four candles and another cigarette. All eyes were upon me. I was center stage and ready to go.

"Hello, everyone," I smiled. "Let's party."

11
AFTERLIFESTYLES OF THE RICH AND NECROTIC

The candle barely scratched the paint off the darkness. I had three more, but morning was still a rumor, and I needed to make them last. As I sat in the foyer facing the balcony, dozens of faces glared all around me. Shadows within shadows loomed like cartoon ink blots trying to blow out the candle with sheer force of will. Now, when I say shadow, I mean a patch of darkness that is not only devoid of light, but also of anything good. Remember as a kid, waking up and seeing that the far corner of your room was darker than the rest? Remember the feeling of dread as you swore you saw it moving? Sometimes you think you heard it breathing in low raspy rumbles. You didn't think something was there, you *knew* it. And it was watching you.

Think about that next time you wake up at 3 a.m.

I shoved the greasy burger wrappers in the bag and tossed it out of the circle. Waves of rage and deep sorrow—and quite frankly—raw insanity, pelted the barrier I made. The energy was so strong I could feel it seeping through. The whole damn place was out to get me. Hours crept by as I sat and reached out with my mind—trying to find a glimmer of hope to latch onto. Something that I could use as a conduit, or if I was real lucky, a stick of dynamite. It was like bobbing for an apple in an Olympic-sized pool full of eels. Imagine sitting in Penn Station during the Christmas season, and everyone is screaming at you—all kinds of anger and hate and theme songs—while a million TVs blasted white noise in surround sound. I was protected, yes, but it still sucked yeti balls.

Suddenly, a spirit presented itself like a car full of coked-up rage clowns with the break line cut. Its contempt was so focused, so absolute, I'd almost say it was pure.

"Come forward, spirit. Present yourself." Above the candle glow a face appeared, gaunt and grooved like it was carved from wood. I recognized him from the pictures Parker gave me.

"Ruiner," the spirit said. His voice sounded like it was being played backwards with a heavy reverb.

"Hello, Ozzy, you old ball bag! How's tricks?" I raised the bottle of whiskey in salute, then took a chug.

"Experiment. Ongoing. Interfere. Do not."

"Sorry, Yoda, but I'm like an honorary Ghost Buster. I can quote the movies *and* the cartoons—not that weak ass shit with the gorilla, mind you..." I lit a cigarette and blew the smoke his way. "And you're forgetting something very important: this is my house now!"

"ENOUGH!" he shouted. The candle blew out, and a slurry of scratches and punches somehow managed to reach me. He was powerful, no denying that. I lit the remaining nub of the first candle and then the second. Faces and hands, clear as day, were so close if they had breath, I'd smell it. The barrier was compromised and beginning to buckle. I emptied the whiskey bottle and set it aflame in blue brilliance. The fire leveled up the barrier like a castle moat. In the spirit world, intent is one of the strongest factors. The power of will is no joke. And another undeniable truth?

Whiskey is magic.

I tossed the empty bottle and started on the second. There had to be a way to clear the house. Then again, the spirits were a cancer that spread through the bones. You can treat it, maybe, but there are times when it's best to just say your goodbyes and punch your own ticket. Sometimes it's better to go out with a bang than a poof. A bang...

The morning came like an underwater car crash, and I had my solution. Light poured in from the windows, shrinking the shadows back to the corners. I needed to leave. That meant leaving the circle—meant being torn to jerky strips by a thousand unseen hands.

"I know how to free you!" I addressed the spirits of the victims. "Help me out and you will be released!" Nothing happened at first. I figured the house had too strong a hold on them. Then, something from a totally 80s metal video happened. The front door burst open like Mike Tyson riding a T-Rex, and shapes appeared to either side of the light like an aisle. I leaped from the circle and felt hands pulling me to the door. I so badly wanted to strut like the boss pimp I was, but before I knew it, I was tossed out on the lawn to the sound of a slamming door. I was safe, and better yet, knew what I needed to do. I staggered to the SUV and started it up.

"I won't fail you," I promised the shapes in the windows and hit the gas.

*

I punched Walker's number in my phone as I rocketed through Gravenfrost. Four rings later, a mumbly, cotton-mouth greeted me.

"Hulluh...?

"Wakey wakey, eggs and bakey, Deputy!"

"Holy shit, Doyle?"

"You were expecting maybe the Easter Bunny?"

"Are you drunk?"

"Inspired. Also yes. I need you and your boys to cordon off the roads leading to The Domicile. Whoever you have blocking Grand Ave, tell 'em to stay frosty."

"What are you planning?"

"Gonna clear that place once and for all, buddy-boy. And you're gonna wanna see this. Just... don't park too close."

"What? Why? What are you—?" I hung up and dialed Parker. This should be a nice finale to his exposé.

"Doyle! Hey!" He was chipper. It was too damn early for chipper.

"You're up?"

"Reporters don't sleep. You okay? How'd it go?"

"Meet Walker by The Domicile."

"At the Domicile. Gotcha."

"*By* The Domicile. Not at. Do not go near it, got me?"

"What's the plan?"

"You remember in *Ghostbusters*, where the containment unit got shut off, and all the ghosts shot through the roof?"

"...Yeah?"

"That was a great scene."

124

"Are you drunk?"

"Also yes." I hung up and cranked the iPod. "Dragula" by Rob Zombie was in order. I hit the PA as I approached Procession Bridge, just to be a dick. The music was good and loud.

Good morning, Gravenfrost.

*

The gods of cockamamie ideas were smiling upon me. Just over the bridge was an Irving gas station. A tanker pulled in as I approached, and the driver exited the cabin and scratched his nuts like a fiend. I came in sliding, and stopped a few feet from him. I jumped out and he stared at me like I was on fire.

"You! Truck monkey! That thing full?"

"The fuck did you just call me?" I pulled my badge and he shrugged.

"FBI, shit toast! I ask again—is that goddamn truck full of go juice?!"

"Yeah, but what's it to you?"

"I need it!"

"You ain't taking my truck, asshole. I got deliveries and also? Fuck you!"

"No time for macho bullshit, citizen!" I ran to the truck. "I have to save the world." He grabbed my arm and threw me down. He wasn't a big dude, but solid as a bran muffin turd.

"You ain't stealing my truck!"

"Obstruction of justice!" I shrieked and punched him in the balls. He doubled over and I gave him a tiger uppercut.

"Police brutality!" shouted a lady who looked like Richard Simmons. A small crowd of early morning commuters had gathered. I opened the driver's door and saluted.

"Lady, I ain't the police, I'm the *gummint!*" I set the truck in gear and tore ass to find a house with a big T on top.

*

"Let me go this instant!" Reverend Clayman hollered as I dragged him from the front doors of Our Lady of Immaculate Deception in his PJs. A bowl of holy water sloshed in my other hand. "How dare you shoot the door to the house of God! How dare you kidnap a—"

"This isn't a kidnapping, Padre," I assured him. I let him go at the tanker and shoved the bowl into his hands. "I need you to bless this tanker." I gave him a thumbs up.

"Are you insane? What am I saying, *of course* you're insane! Why would anyone need to bless a petroleum truck?"

"Because I'm going to use it to blow The Devil's Domicile to kingdom crap."

"Really?"

"Yep!"

"Good! Screw that place!" he cheered.

"I'm glad you see it my way, Padre! I need you to shimmy up the ladder there, and give the truck a good fire and brimstone exorcism blessing, okay?"

"Alright!" He clambered up the ladder after me, and stood near the hatch I opened. He held the bowl up and closed his eyes. "O' Heavenly Father, please cast your blessings upon this tanker truck, that it may act as your fiery sword, Lord, and strike against The Devil's Domicile! Allow this blessed holy water to transform the petrol within into your divine napalm! Aid this crazy man to remove that blight from your kingdom! By The Father, The Son, The Holy Ghost, and The Archangel

Michael, let it be so!" He poured the water in.

"Amen and hot damn!" I slapped his shoulder. We climbed down and shook hands. "Thank you, Padre!" I got behind the wheel and lowered the window.

"Go with God, my son. And I expect you will pay for the door?"

"Jesus was a carpenter, so..." I waved and took off in my holy torpedo. I smiled when I saw the Padre flipping me off in the rear view.

*

As I barreled down Grand Avenue, I cackled with maniacal glee at every police sawhorse I smashed through. The Domicile lurched up like a Toho Monster, and I saw Parker and Walker standing by the gate just like I told them *not* to.

Dopes.

I held the horn down. They scrambled behind the Winnebago across the street like a couple of dumbfounded roaches. I had to time it right. Get through the iron gate without losing momentum or control, and make it as far into the house as possible. Oh, and jump out somewhere along the way.

Piece of cake.

I hit the gate and sent the bars flying. Back and forth the truck swerved—I struggled to keep it from capsizing and grinding to a halt before it reached the house. Lucky for me, it reached the house quickly. Unlucky for me, I had no time to jump. The sound was deafening as I crashed through the front of the house and into the stairs. The floor gave way and the truck teetered and plunged hard into the basement. I woke up in the truck, laying on a bed of shattered windshield and debris. I half expected to be drowning in gasoline, but somehow the tank was still intact.

"Doyle! You alive?" Walker shouted.

"Stay back! I got this!" I grabbed the wheel and slowly pulled myself up. I opened the door, which damn near fell off the hinge. "I got this," I assured myself. I tumbled from the cabin and pressed myself against the side. The dead were all around me and sorely pissed. Quickest route up would have been the stairs leading to the kitchen, but I knew I'd be murderized as soon as I left the protection of my God bomb. That left me one choice: climb. So I did. Battered, bloody, and freshly hungover, I slowly made my way up the side of the tanker to the foyer. I rolled from the crumbling hole and stared up at the horrific face of Oswald Dickinson. His features were disjointed and hateful.

"Ruiner!"

"Yeah, yeah, blow it out your ass." Cold hands grabbed me again like frozen lumberjacks. Their features were more distinct now. The house was losing its grip on them. I recognized some of the people lifting me up from the photos. Their wounds weren't as profound as they once were. As they pulled me to the opening, I could swear I saw some of them smiling. Off I went again, sailing from the house and into the loving embrace of a lawn full of bricks and assorted hard shit. Walker pulled me to the street where two EMTs rushed over. I shooed them away and noticed the gathering crowd of onlookers.

"What are you doing?" Walker asked. "You're bleeding."

"Ain't got time to bleed." I cough-chuckled.

"But you are. Let the EMTs look at you."

"We aren't done. Show's not over." I pulled both guns out.

"The hell are you doing?" Parker asked.

"Gonna stab the devil with his own pitchfork."

"The hell does that even mean?"

"Dunno, sounded cool though." I wiped blood from my eyes. "Alright, fellas, grab yer guns. We're gonna have us an exorcism."

"That's your solution? Shooting a gas truck?!" Walker wasn't amused.

"The gas is blessed."

"Why do I believe you?"

"Because I'm the man!" We fired into the tanker until our guns were dry. Gas gushed out like a Vegas water show. The first responders and onlookers cheered.

"Nothing happened..." Parker stated with a hint of *aww, maaaan*.

"This isn't the movies, pal. Walker, pop your trunk." I was actually relieved that he'd parked so close. I didn't feel like limping that far. I rummaged through the trunk and pulled out a bullhorn and a beautiful, bright orange flare gun. I shoved the bullhorn at Walker. "Tell everybody to get back."

"You're insane!" Parker laughed out of shock and the need to see something explode.

"Hush up when grown folks are working. Walker? Hop-to."

"Everyone move back!" He shouted. "Back! Go home, even! Get these squad cars up the road, dammit!" The emergency vehicles ushered the crowds back. Parker drove the 'Bago down the road and stood near it. Walker, on the other hand, stayed put.

"You better bug out too, Bruce." I elbowed his arm.

"No. I need to see this."

"You'll see it from space. I'm not doing a damn thing until you get the hell away. I'll hide behind the ambulance. I'll be fine, but not if you get hurt."

"I didn't know you cared."

"I don't. I just know Annie would stomp out my lungs if anything happened to you." We shook hands, and he drove his car over to Parker. I gripped the flare gun and stared at the house like an old West showdown. Shapes of victims and villains appeared, waiting to be free. I tried to think of something cool to say for the movie adaption—because there *will* be one—but nothing came to mind. I aimed the gun and fired.

FOOMP!

The flare sailed in slow motion. It was almost hypnotic. So much, in fact, that I forgot to run. The explosion threw me like an action figure into the side of the ambulance. Scores of cursing stones were embedded like shrapnel around me. And, lo and behold, inside me too. I laughed when I saw the rock protruding from my gut like that little guy from *Total Recall*. Squato, or Reggie, or whatever his name was. Shock is a funny thing. Orbs of brilliant blue and white soared and swirled on the flames, and rose skyward. It was truly one of the most serene moments of my life.

"Just like... *Ghostbusters*." I whispered proudly. A charred body crashed to the street several feet away with a crispy thud. "Heya, Chuck!" I laughed harder, and felt the burning in my gut. Emergency vehicles swarmed. Walker rushed the EMTs my way, and was startled when he saw me.

"Doyle, you okay?! Oh, hell, he's bleeding bad! Get in there guys!" He ordered the medics.

"Don't let the firefighters fire... fight." I muttered. The world was growing dark. I was checking out. The last victim of The Devil's Domicile. I could live with that.

Die with that.

Whatever.

"Jesus!" Parker shouted, as we watched the foundation give way and pull the remains of the house back down to Hell. The medics put me on a gurney and wheeled it around the debris toward the ambulance. A massive sucking noise filled the air. The flames and smoke retreated underground, and everyone braced for an explosion. Instead, the hole crumbled into itself until the massive crater was full of blackened dirt and bad memories.

"I'm pretty awesome." I managed to say before the lights went out.

12
HAPPINESS IS A CUP OF BLACK COFFEE AT THE END OF THE WORLD

"And where do you think you're going, honey?" Nurse Pearl Jones folded her meaty arms across her meaty chest, and blocked the door to my hospital room.

"Things to do, my love," I said, trying to pull my tattered and singed jacket on.

"Honey, you've been blown half to hell, smashed, bashed, cut up, *and* concussed. The only thing you got to do is get your white ass back in bed and heal."

"I appreciate all the sponge baths, Pearl, but I'm just not ready for a commitment." I limped over to her and rested my head on her shoulder. "It was beautiful while it lasted."

"You're crazy," she laughed, and stepped aside.

"Gifted," I corrected, and limped down the hall. The elevator door opened with perfect timing, revealing the dumbfounded faces of my two minions.

"The hell are you doing?" Walker took me by the arm and juggled the idea of dragging me back to my room.

"I'm good. Ready to roll."

"He's good." Parker scoffed. "You've been in the hospital for a week, most of which you were unconscious for, and you're good?"

"That's right, smartass. I got a promise to keep to Zane Bagley. I'm gonna get him some real help far away from that craptastic asylum."

"Fine," Walker conceded. "But first, food."

"Grant's?" Parker asked.

"Grant's" I smiled. We got back in the elevator and hit the lobby button. "Any word from the Bureau?"

"I called them to let them know what happened. They said they'll send someone to collect Hobbs and Waifly. They also said to tell you to 'Get well someday'. They don't like you, do they?"

"Not particularly."

"Oh!" Parker exclaimed, and reached into his stupid trench coat. "We got you a little something." He handed me a palm-sized box with duck wrapping paper.

"Thanks, you guys."

"Open it." Parker beamed.

"Really? Is that how presents work?"

"Don't be a dick, Doyle." Walker shook his head. "I know that's like asking the sun not to rise, though."

"You're learning!" I smiled. I opened the box and plucked out a flat stone with Agent Doyle scratched into it.

"That's your curse stone," Walker said. "One of Hobbs's turd burglars must have made it when you started making moves on their mistress."

"And guess where it was found!" said Parker.

"Where?"

"Right there," he pointed to my stomach. "A thousand bricks and rocks and it was *that* one that found its way to you."

"What can I say?" I stared at the rock that nearly

ended me. What *could* I say?

*

We entered Grant's Diner to a round of applause. The locals were grateful that they had one less bump in the night to deal with. We sat at a window booth, and Annie filled our cups with beautiful black liquid. She kissed Walker and smiled.

"How you feeling, Special?" I took a sip of the magic elixir and rubbed the thick stubble on my cheek.

"Let's see, I was drugged, beaten, unsuccessfully possessed, mauled by ghosts, car-crashed, exploded, AND stabbed in the gut by a rock with my name on it. But I *did* get laid, so I'm aces. How about you, Bruce? How you feeling after, you know...?"

"I'm okay." He smiled and took Annie's hand. "For once in a long time, I feel whole. We saved lives. We broke the cycle of death. No, you know what? I'm feeling pretty damn good!" He kissed Annie. "And you, man! You broke the house! You set them free... set— *him*—free. I can't thank you enough."

"We set them free. I couldn't have done it without you jokers. How about you, Parker? How's our roving reporter?"

"Got my story, got my life, got to pistol-whip an asshole to a bloody pulp. Hell, I haven't had this much fun in a long time!" he laughed. "Looks like I'll have to move on, though. Once I publish this piece, this place'll be crawling with mobsters. That's not good for me or the town."

"You know what? You should go to O'Connor's Pub in Brooklyn, see a woman by the name of Whiskey Rose." Parker looked at me like I told him to floss with a chainsaw.

"I'm not going to the lion's den for a cocktail,

man."

"Yeah, no. She's also in witness protection. Well, was. She's a bio-plastique specialist who can make masks so real it'd blow your mind. She can make you look like whoever you want! You can move around freely again. She does some freelance work for the Bureau from time to time."

"What do you mean, she *was* in witness protection?" Walker cocked an eyebrow.

"She joined a gang called The Ghoulie Girls. That, and the people coming after her kind of... stopped breathing."

"You ever use her masks?" Parker asked.

"And cover up *this* face? Ha! No way, pally. I just send people who need to hide to her. If you do go, tell her I sent you. If she doesn't stab you in the neck, she'll help you out."

"Well, breakfast is on me," Annie smiled. "Prepare for a ton of eggs, meat, and assorted starchy goodness." She brushed Walker's ear and went to get the food. That's when I saw him. The mystery son of a bitch that was making me think I was losing my mind. Right there in the corner booth, reading a newspaper and sipping coffee.

"Sonuvabitch," I whispered. The fellas looked confused as I slowly stood and limped over to him. I slid into the booth and let out a pained breath despite myself. "Hey."

"Hello," he said. His eyes never left the paper. His voice was deep like a narrator. It fit his hulking form.

"Something you want to say to me?"

"I'm sorry?" He looked up. His eyes were those of a man who had seen some shit. Strong eyes—the eyes of a gladiator or a general.

"You were in the graveyard, and the bus stop."

"Is it possible I was visiting a loved one who has

135

passed and that I take mass transit?" His eyes sank back to the paper.

> Infuriating asshole.
> Is that what *I'm* like?
> Stop nodding.

"No, that doesn't add up. I trust my gut, and my gut says you're here for me. You got something going on, and I want to know what it is. You need me to pull my badge on you to make it official business?"

"Please do." He folded the paper. I tossed my badge on the paper and tried to look tough. Truth was, I was in no shape for a confrontation with a giant. He reached into his coat and my asshole could have turned coal into diamonds. He set two black leather badge holders next to mine.

"What's...?"

"My name is Simon Bradshaw." He unfolded the first badge. It was black with raised silver writing. *Bradshaw*, it said. DSI.

"Yeah, right," I half laughed, half wheeze-gasped. "Black badge? DSI? I'm a nut hair away from placing you under arrest."

"You have heard of the DSI, yes?" he asked. His tone never wavered.

"The Department of Special Investigation? Yeah, it's a water cooler crank-yanker that a bunch of super nerds concocted to make them seem cool and super-secrety. They say the 'Special' is really 'Supernatural.' It's all conjecture. DSI is just another hum-drum federal entity."

"All you've seen and you still question?"

"Damn right."

"That's why you've been chosen. The Department works in tandem with the FBI and the CIA, handling the cases neither are equipped to handle.

According to your record, you'd be a perfect fit." He opened the second badge. It looked just like his, but with my last name on it.

"Bullshit," I said. Bradshaw produced a cell phone and hit a button. Once the call connected, he handed it over.

"Hello?"

"Doyle? How you doing, my boy?"

"Director Cook? Wh-what's going on here?"

"Opportunity, kiddo! You're a fine agent. A little strange, but effective. But as your supervisor, I strongly suggest you take Mr. Bradshaw up on his offer. This is a huge step, son."

"Yes... sir."

"Helluva job you did in Gravenfrost. Damn fine."

"Thank you, sir."

"Ha-ha, it's just Ted now. You'll be in a different league. I'd imagine I'd have to call *you* sir now. Ha-ha. Take care, son. And don't drop the ball on this one!" He hung up and I handed the phone back.

"Do I have a choice?"

"This is America, Agent Doyle. You can do whatever you like. I only ask that you truly consider joining us. We do some amazing things for Mankind."

"Yeah?" I laughed. "Like what?"

"Like keeping them alive." He smiled. "There are so many things you've yet to learn about the world, about the balance that must be maintained for things to run smoothly. I think—no—I *know* you would make a great addition to the Order."

"Order?"

"*Department.*" He put his badge away and pointed to my old shield. "One is existing." He pointed to the DSI badge. "The other is living. Experiencing what the world truly is, and making a difference. A real, tangible difference—not just in rhetoric."

"How's the pay?"

"Ridiculously high. You will work for it, though."

"You saw me blow a house up?"

"I did."

"Then you know I'll do whatever needs doing."

"I have no doubt. I'm also confident that it won't be the last house you demolish." He smiled. I picked up the new badge and studied it. Up until now, the DSI seemed like a bunch of nerds that created a mystique to help them get laid—but I could sense Bradshaw was legit. Hell... what have I got to lose? I slid both badges into my jacket pocket and gave it a tap.

"Alright. I'm in."

Bradshaw nodded happily and shook my hand. "Congratulations, Special Agent Doyle. Welcome to the bigger picture." I lifted myself up and zombie-shuffled back over to my table. I quickly looked back to see if Bradshaw had pulled another Batman on me, but he simply lifted his coffee cup and winked.

"What happened?" Parker asked. I slumped back into my seat and showed them my new badge.

"I think I just got a promotion."

13
FAIR THEE WELL, SWEET PRINCES OF MAINE

Outside the Gravenfrost Asylum for the Cheerful and Generally Happy to Be There, I buckled Zane Bagley into the passenger seat of the SUV. I could feel the tension in him release as I did.

"You sure you don't want to cuff him?" Walker said. Annie handed me a take-out bag full of tasty diner love, which I placed on Zane's lap.

"Don't screw that, now." I winked. Zane laughed for the first time in what I'd bet was a while. "Naw, Zane's alright. Right?"

"Yes, sir," he stated, more timidly than his muscular frame was accustomed to. "I feel like I'm myself again... mostly."

"See? Mostly is good enough for me! We'll get you some help far away from here. Your show still sucks, though."

"No more show," he said into the bag of intoxicating wonder-stink.

"Good call." I closed his door. Parker pulled up

in the 'Bago, and hopped out with Bukowski in tow.

"All good?" He nodded.

"All good."

"Damn right," Walker added. "We destroyed The Domicile, saved a few kids from certain doom, put a couple of devil-worshiping dickholes behind bars and one in the ground. I think that qualifies as all good."

"*Dickholes*?" Annie chuckled. "God, you're even starting to talk like him."

"Sincerest form of flattery," I winked.

"Oh, that reminds me!" Walker snapped his fingers. "Mrs. Gibblin has been calling the station, wanting to thank us for freeing her from her anal polyp son."

"Oh?" I laughed. "She bake a cake? Maybe some granny cookies?"

"No. She offered a spit roast." Walker grimaced. I gagged.

"What? That's really nice!" Annie shrugged, confused. "What, like a suckling pig or a turkey?"

"Oh, honey, you don't know?" Walker pursed his lips.

"Know what?"

"Doyle?" Walker looked to me, but I spiked the ball right back.

"Oh, hell no, Deputy. You brought it up, you knock it down."

"A spit roast..." Walker rubbed his eyes and sighed. "Is when two guys have... sex with a woman who is on all fours, you know, doggy style... one in the mouth and the other... w-well..." He pressed the tips of his index fingers together. Annie stared at us like we just Lady-and-the-Tramped a dog turd.

"UGH! And you *know* what that is, Bruce? I expected Special to, but...wow!"

"Later, ask him what a chili dog is." I winked. Walker slapped his forehead. "Now that I've done a

satisfying amount of property—and now marital—
damage, I should hit the road."

"Thanks for not arresting me for evidence
tampering." Parker and I shook hands.

"Remember: Brooklyn, O'Connor's, Whiskey
Rose."

"Right. Soon as I publish this piece, I'm going to
head out. Maybe I'll hit there first, as I am positive the
mob will head here. Sorry, Walker."

"Hey, they start any shit, I'll handle it. I've never
seen you before. Parker *who*?" He laughed.

"You mean Aquaman?" Annie joked. "Oh, I'm
so gonna throw you under the bus." Parker feigned being
stabbed in the heart. "As for you, Special..." she gave me
a big hug and a kiss on the cheek. "Thank you."

"Don't mention it, beautiful. Homeys look out
for homeys." I turned to Bukowski. "Ready, pal?" He
shook his tail, but didn't budge from Parker's side.

"Go ahead, buddy." Parker urged. Bukowski
trotted back inside the 'Bago and plopped his ass down.
"Um..."

"I can take a hint!" I yelled at the dog. "Looks
like you got a road buddy. If you want him."

"You-you don't mind?"

"Way I see it, you two get along pretty well, and
with my new position, I might be running all over the
damn place. It's not fair to him to keep dragging him
along. He's yours if you want him. Hell, maybe I'll get a
cat... or two."

"Alright, man, thanks!" We shook hands again.

"I can't convince you to stick around a while,
can I? The Domicile isn't the only show in town. And
looks like we're gonna have some Goombah troubles,
thanks to Parker."

"If it's any consolation, I'm sure the nature of my
new job will bring me through here again. I'm a phone
call away, too. Not that I answer my phone, but you

know, sentiment." We shook hands and laughed. "Be good, Sheriff."

"Sheriff?"

"You'll see." I waved and got into the car. It was time to put some distance between me, Zane and that crazy-ass town. If I live long enough, I might retire there —who knows? I wonder if Mack will hang my picture next to Godzilla on the wall of famous people. Zane rested his head against the window, and watched the graveyard town shrink in the rear view.

"You know what bugs the crap out of me?" I said, as we made our way across Procession Bridge.

"What?" Zane kept his eyes to the past. The sound of the metal lattice bridge hummed throughout the cabin.

"Thirty six. I still don't get the significance. All I heard was: *Thirty six! Bleh! Thirty six! Rar!* But what the hell, you know?"

"It's retarded easy," Zane shrugged.

"Keep in mind, I'm now, like a 007 or something —I don't have to take no lip from no shitty TV host. I'll throw your ass in the trunk... that's open to the back seat, so, never mind." I lit a cigarette. "Alright, smart guy, what's the deal with thirty six?"

"Thirty six. Three. Six. Three Sixes. Six. Six. Six."

"That's stupid," I puffed.

"See? Retarded easy." Zane went back to wherever he goes now. I felt the pull of Gravenfrost like a loose sweater thread, and the weight of my new badge grow heavier and heavier with every mile.

ARR: THAT'S IT?
ARD: ISN'T THAT ENOUGH?
ARR: THEN WHAT HAPPENED?
ARD: I CAME HERE. ZANE GOT PLUCKED BY OUR BRAIN-MEN, AND I HAD THE PRIVELEGE OF STARING AT YOU FOR THE PAST FEW

HOURS. THE AGENCY IS SENDING A FUN
WAGON FOR HOBBS AND WAIFLY, AND YOU
AND I ARE ABOUT TO GO GET DRINKS.
ARR: SO, THIS NEW POSITION... WE
AREN'T TECHNICALLY CO-WORKERS ANYMORE,
RIGHT? YOU DON'T ANSWER TO DIRECTOR
COOK ANYMORE?
ARD: FAR AS I CAN TELL, THIS
DEBRIEFING IS MY LAST OFFICIAL FBI
BUSINESS.
ARR: IN THAT CASE, LET'S GET THAT
DRINK.
ARD: YOU KNOW, THIS COULD BE THE
BEGINNING OF A BEAUTIFUL REGRET.
ARR: SHUT UP, GRAB YOUR COAT, AND PASS
ME A CIGARETTE.
ARD: A BEAUTIFUL REGRET.

[SOUND OF DOOR CLOSING]

[RECORDER PICKING UP INCREASED AMBIENT
WHITE NOISE]

MULTIPLE UNIDENTIFIED VOICES:
INDISTINCT CHATTER. MENACING HOWLS AND
SHRIEKS.
UNIDENTIFIED DISTINCT VOICE: BOBBY...
BONES...
UNIDENTIFIED DISTINCT VOICE: RUINER!

[RECORDING ENDS]

SUGGESTED LISTENING

"Dragula" by Rob Zombie
"Children of the Grave" by Black Sabbath
"Peace Frog" by The Doors
"12 Black Rainbows" by Type O Negative
"Without End" by Dommin
"(I Don't Need You To) Set Me Free" by
Grinderman
"Shadow of Death Hotel" by Barry Adamson
"Bury You Now, Dig You Later" by The Memphis
Morticians
"Pinhead" by The Ramones
"Gimme Shelter" by The Rolling Stones
"Fear is All You Know" by King Dude
"Red Right Hand" by Nick Cave and the Bad Seeds
"The Kids Who Want to Play With the Dead" by
Lordi

Also, the entire Kreeps discography. Specifically:
"SuperNova," "Leather & Bone," "Saltair,"
"Voodoo Black Exorcist," "Geekula," "Cyanide,"
"Days Like These," "You're Gonna Ruin That
Girl." Find them at kreepsmusic.com.

ABOUT THE AUTHOR

Peter Hammarberg is a scruffy-looking word herder
dwelling in the northern wilds of New England.
He's been called a "Magnificent Bastard" and "The
Patron Saint of Bourbon and Hearty Laughter" by
genuine Coney Island sideshow performers. He is
the author of the sci-fi novel, *Antillia*. For more,
visit: hammermountainarts.com or
hammarblog.wordpress.com.

32890752R00085